THE BEST

DEATH

Written by Shalina Casey

Angry Eagle Publishing
AngryEaglePublishing.com

THE WONDERS OF LIFE

At times, we may experience profound despair, seeing life and the world as utterly devoid of value, overwhelmed by intense pain that can overshadow everything else, leading to a state of desperation where hope can feel like a distant memory. However, through unexpected acts of courage, life can change. In the still of darkness, a sparkle of light could reveal the hidden beauty and possibilities, causing the once all-encompassing pain to recede. The weight on our shoulders lightens, and the magnificence and potential that surrounds us becomes visible. Simple acts of kindness, connections with others, or the realisation that there's still much to live for serve as a reminder that even during painful times, hope exists.

In this world we live in, everyone has unique stories, struggles, and victories. Sometimes we briefly cross paths and become a small part of each other's stories. Other times, we stay strangers, connected only by sharing a moment in time.

Every person we meet carries their life of

experiences, feelings, and dreams. As we journey through this life, we meet others, sometimes it's by chance. A quick meeting, a short talk, or a shared smile can leave a strong impression, changing our perceptions, giving us a brief moment of joy, or an uplifting break from our challenges. These interactions and meetings can remind us that we are all connected and that our actions can have a huge impact on others and vice versa, even if we don't realise it at the time.

There are also countless people we will never meet, strangers with whom we share this world with. We might walk past them on the street, sit near them on a bus, or stand in the same line, never knowing their experiences or struggles. In the end, within our shared humanity, we are connected by the ups and downs that shape our lives.

If ever you find yourself in the depths of hopelessness, hold on to the possibility that life will change. The world may yet reveal its magic to you, and if it does, you will discover that your worth is far greater than you ever imagined.

This story will present you with a range of complex and difficult events, exploring a group of characters who commit themselves to a transformative journey, where they uncover the profound meaning behind these words.

As they steer through the twists and

turns of their experiences, their lives are forever altered. The familiar world they once knew undergoes a remarkable shift, revealing itself to be nothing more than a semblance of what they thought was real. In this newfound realisation, the present time seems to dissolve into a realm that no longer holds any factual existence. The characters are confronted with the fragility of their perceptions and are compelled to question the very meaning of their reality. Through this revelation they are challenged to redefine their understanding of the world and their place within it.

CONTENTS

Dedication

This book is in memory of my beautiful, kind, and wonderful Mother, Tina Casey. 1956-2020.

SHALINA CASEY

PROLOGUE

~THE AIRPORT~

Stepping into Stansted International Airport, the exterior gleams in the sunlight, inviting you to embark on a journey of exploration. Inside, the swarming atmosphere and vibrant surroundings create a feeling of excitement and efficiency, fuelling anticipation for the adventures that lie ahead. Every detail, flawlessly crafted, creating a spirit of travel and discovery, making Stansted International an unforgettable gateway to new experiences.

It's September 2030, a peculiar warmth envelopes the day, setting an unusual tone for a midday Thursday. The sun's descent paints the landscape in a rich, golden light, stirring an uncomplicated sense of excitement in the atmosphere. Unbeknownst to the hectic crowd within the airport, this day holds the promise of becoming a pivotal moment in history, one that will etch itself into the collective memory as a transformative event.

As travellers navigate through the airport's lively aerodrome, they carry with them a tapestry of aspirations, ambitions, and the allure of the unknown. Amidst the bustling terminals, a world of boundless opportunities unfurled, beckoning them to embark on journeys that will lead them to destinations both familiar and distant, each step paves the way for new horizons to be explored and cherished.

The terminal is buzzing with life and excitement; a sensory symphony of aromas follow each person moving through the lively airport. Cafes exude the rich scent of freshly brewed coffee while the food courts tease the nose with international flavours blending in the air. The subtle hint of perfume adds to the atmosphere of anticipation.

Throughout the terminal, various amenities catered to the needs of travellers. Cafes and restaurants beckoned with their tantalising menus, offering a global culinary experience.

Duty-free shops enticed passersby with luxurious

goods, souvenirs, and the promise of tax-free shopping. Lounges provide a haven for premium travellers, which offer comfort, privacy, and complimentary luxuries. Moving walkways whisk passengers effortlessly through the terminal, their smooth motion reminiscent of a gentle river current guiding them along their journey. The sound of rolling suitcases echoes through the corridors like a chorus of distant thunder creating a rhythm that mirrors the heartbeat of the airport. The departure gates themselves are like portals to another world. Large floor-to-ceiling windows offer panoramic views of the tarmac, where planes stand like majestic creatures ready to take flight. The air is permeated with the smell of jet fuel, blending with the odour of nervous excitement from the travellers.

Above, a network of steel beams and cables stretched across the ceiling, reminiscent of a spider's intricate web. The skylights in between allowed streaks of sunlight to filter through, casting warm rays that danced upon the polished floors below. The terminal seems to breathe, alive with the hum of conversations, the beeping of scanners, and the distant roar of engines.

In the end, the airport is a metaphor for the

threshold between the ordinary and the extraordinary. It is a liminal space where dreams and desires of individuals gather, where the surreal could potentially manifest in the most unexpected ways. As the travellers venture forth into the mysterious areas before them, their lives hold the possibility of being forever changed, their perspectives expanded by the boundless wonders that lay beyond the confines of the known world.

There are times when journeys are not undertaken for the purpose of fun, business, or relaxation. At unexpected moments, they are thrust upon individuals by an unforeseen twist of fate, which could perhaps transpire into a sequence of unobtrusive events.

In this particular instance, a group of strangers find themselves setting off on a path that could possibly intersect at a pivotal moment of extraordinary discoveries. Each of these individuals carries burdens and dreams. As their journey unfolds, little do they realise the profound impact they would have on one another's lives.

CHAPTER 1

~*THE AIRPORT BAR* ~

Dave Wilson, a 49-year-old man, is desolate and lonely. The loss of his job as an IT technician has left him adrift. He resides in a solitary state, occupying a council terraced house in Hackney, London. Dave's attire consisted of a black leather jacket and jeans, combined with dishevelled hair and unshaven face, reflecting his neglected appearance. However, there was a bewildering charm and attractiveness that was somewhat concealed by his shabby outward presentation. He tortured his mind with the inability to achieve things like punctuality and simple instructions.

He felt inferior to others which had a detrimental effect on his achievements. He desperately yearned for love or even just to connect with another soul. Dave spent many years feeling lost and alone contemplating his current plans which included abandoning his life altogether.

Sitting at a table outside a foyer bar with a pint and casually watching the crowds of people walk by. Dave carefully took in his surroundings, noticing the vibrant atmosphere of the airport. The hustle and bustle of people rushing to catch their flights contrasted with the relaxed pace of those who had time to spare. It felt like a microcosm of life where some were in a perpetual rush, driven by deadlines and responsibilities, while others savoured each moment, embracing a more leisurely approach. As Dave continued his observation, he noticed families swarming through the airport with children brimming with excitement. The little ones eagerly pulled their suitcases along, their eyes filled with joy.

The families moved swiftly, determined to reach their departure gates before the clock ticked down. In this flurry of activity, the airport became a hub of energy, as parents guided their children through the mass of corridors and security checkpoints. Some shared moments of suspense, exchanging glances and whispered conversations, perhaps discussing their upcoming adventures or the thrill of exploring new destinations together. Others found themselves bidding farewell, their goodbyes tinged with a bittersweet sense of longing.

In the space of transitions, emotions ran high, creating a mood charged with eagerness, joy, and sometimes included moments of sadness. It was a place where connections were formed and broken, where paths intersected briefly before diverging once again. The airport served as a cosmos of the individual experiences, highlighting the ebb and flow of relationships and the emotions which accompanied the act of moving from one place to another.

Within the airport, Dave also noticed a plethora of shops, bars, and food court areas, all designed to cater to the diverse needs and preferences of travellers. Some individuals discovered relief in the act of retail therapy, leisurely strolling through the stores, perusing shelves filled with souvenirs, or indulging in the allure of luxury items. In addition to the shopping experience, the airport provided spaces where people could find quiet intervals from the hectic pace of travel. Cafes and bars attracted groups of individuals seeking a moment of relaxation or socialisation. They gathered around tables, savouring a well-deserved drink or enjoying a quick snack.

Dave found comfort in the airport's ambiance. He was engrossed in people watching, exploring his interest in observing the unique interactions and behaviours of fellow travellers. He appreciated the diversity of cultures, languages, and fashion styles that converged in this busy global hub. In this transient environment, Dave was a mere observer, a passenger passing through, absorbing the energy and dynamics of the airport. He had the choice to join the rush or embrace the slower pace, taking his time to explore the various amenities and to accept his own fate in this unorthodox journey. Instead he found solidarity in sipping his pint of lager at the airport bar.

A couple at the table next to Dave tried hard to get his attention. Dave turned his head towards the couple and met their gazes. He eventually noticed their attempts to grab his attention and realised they needed something. Curiosity piqued, he smiled warmly and said, "Hi."

The couple explained that they were celebrating their anniversary and would like someone to take a photo of them together. They asked Dave if he would be kind enough to help them capture the moment. Dave's face lit up with genuine delight as he responded, "Yes, sure."

He stood up from his table and walked over to join the couple. They handed him their camera, and Dave took a moment to familiarise himself with the device's settings. After ensuring everything was set correctly, he guided the couple into a nice pose, making sure they were framed well in the shot. Dave took a few photos, capturing different angles and moments to give the couple a variety of options. He paid attention to details like lighting and composition, aiming to capture the essence of their celebration. Once he felt satisfied with the shots, he handed back the camera to the couple. "Here you go! I hope these photos turn out good. Happy anniversary!"

The couple expressed their gratitude, thanking Dave for his kindness. With a smile, he nodded and returned to his table, happy to have been able to contribute to their special day. The couple asked Dave if he was off to Tenerife. When he told them he was going to Sweden, they smiled with enthusiasm, informing him that they had never been there. As the conversation continued, it became evident that the couple had limited knowledge about Sweden. Dave also knew very little about the country.

Realising the conversation had hit a temporary lull, Dave smiled and nodded at the couple's interest in Sweden. As they inquired about the weather, Dave hesitated for a moment, unsure about the specific climate in Sweden at that time. He replied honestly, "I'm not entirely sure about the weather in Sweden right now."

An awkward silence briefly dampened the initial encounter, as neither Dave nor the couple seemed to have anything further to add to the conversation.

Dave and his younger sister Jenny had a challenging upbringing within the fostering system. At the ages of five and three respectively, their birth parents went out to celebrate their second-year anniversary, a rare occasion for their parents to have some time for themselves. However, tragedy struck when their parents were involved in a fatal car accident. Due to Dave's unrecognised and misunderstood behaviours, he was frequently shuffled from one foster family to another. On the other hand, Jenny was more reserved and always aimed to please others.

Unfortunately, when Dave was seven and Jenny was five, they were placed in separate homes, further complicating their already difficult situation. Years later, when Dave was nineteen and Jenny was seventeen, they finally reunited. They attempted to confront their shared past and find healing together.

Their efforts only seemed to reopen old wounds and cause more pain. They led different lives and had grown apart over time. Despite this, they would exchange the occasional text message to maintain some level of connection.

Dave took another sip from his glass, savouring the remnants of his pint, his mind drifting to the vastness of the world that lay before him. Feeling a sense of curiosity and wonder, Dave finished his pint in a final gulp, setting his glass down on the table. It was time to embark on his own journey. Picking up his hand luggage, he made his way to the newsagents, a place where he could gather some reading material for his upcoming flight.

As he perused the shelves, he browsed through the vast variety of stories, perspectives, and knowledge that existed in the world. From travel magazines showcasing exotic destinations to newspapers reporting on current events, each publication held a glimpse into the lives and narratives of people near and far. With a sense of anticipation, Dave selected a few publications that caught his eye, eager to delve into the stories within. He knew that through these written words, he would gain insights into different cultures, learn about the challenges and triumphs of individuals, and perhaps even find inspiration for his journey. Leaving the newsagents, Dave headed towards his gate.

He was aware that this adventure was not about visiting a new place. He had made a conscious choice to start again. A narrative which excluded the person he was now.

CHAPTER 2

~THE AIRPORT FRAGRANCE SHOP~

Manjit Pojab, aged 38, was a character who embodied the image of a successful businesswoman. She lived in Chelsea, a vibrant neighbourhood in London known for its upscale residences and thriving business community. Manjit was of Indian descent and possessed a strikingly beautiful appearance with shiny bobbed black hair accentuating her features. Her hair added to her overall aura of confidence and sophistication enhancing the image she presented to the world. Manjit's physical appearance was just one aspect of her multifaceted personality which was shaped by her accomplishments in the business world and her determination to succeed.

At first glance, she seemed to have it all together. However, beneath her polished exterior lay a hidden secret and a sense of bitter resentment. Manjit was sharply assertive, often coming across as intimidating to those around her. She thrived on being in control, particularly when it came to her appearance. She had a clear understanding of her preferences and was fortunate enough to have the means to acquire what she desired.

Despite her achievements, there was a deep longing within Manjit for something more meaningful in her life. She yearned for a sense of purpose and fulfilment but struggled to break free from the constraints of her current existence. Uncertain of how to navigate her desire for change, she found herself caught in a state of internal conflict.

Manjit walked through the shopping mall with her mum, Sudi Pojab. Sudi, aged 65, boasted a graceful appearance with her grey hair. Despite her age, she maintained a remarkable level of wellness that was evident in her demeanour. Adorned in a beautiful churidar, she emanated elegance and charm. Sudi's attire enhanced her overall appearance, accentuating her grace and style. Her choice of clothing reflected her refined taste and appreciation for traditional aesthetics. Sudi was a testament to the fact that age was no barrier to looking and feeling fabulous, as she effortlessly carried herself with poise and confidence.

Sudi was a character who beamed care and gentleness. Her sole desire was to see her daughter thrive and experience the best that life had to offer. Sudi personified kindness and consideration in her every action and interaction. She consistently went out of her way to ensure the well-being and happiness of those around her, particularly Manjit. Her nurturing nature and genuine concern for others was apparent in everything she did. Sudi was a source of tremendous support and a beacon of warmth in Manjit's life.

Manjit's eyes caught sight of a charming fragrance shop. "Mum, let's look in here," she insisted, tugging at her mother's arm. Sudi glanced at the perfume shop, unsure why Manjit was so determined to look for perfume. She couldn't care less about shopping so she tried to pull Manjit away. But Manjit insisted she wanted to buy some expensive perfume and to try on the latest fragrances. Sudi made it clear that she wasn't really in the mood, to which Manjit became emotional and pleaded with her mother to just do what they normally would for a couple of days. Sudi called to mind Manjit's reasons and swiftly agreed.

Manjit embraced her mother, linking arms and resting her head on her shoulder, "You're the most amazing mum a girl could ever ask for." She kissed her mum's cheek, "I love you. Now, let's buy some perfume and make this day special." Sudi smiled, feeling the warmth of her daughter's love and strength.

As Manjit and Sudi entered the fragrance shop, they were welcomed by a delightful blend of scents. The shelves were lined with colourful bottles of various shapes and sizes, each containing a unique fragrance waiting to be discovered. Manjit's eyes lit up with excitement as she scanned the shelves, eager to find the perfect perfume. Sudi, although initially reluctant, couldn't help but be drawn into her daughter's enthusiasm. She began exploring the different fragrances alongside Manjit. Allowing herself to be immersed in the experience, she sprayed test strips with different perfumes, taking in the intoxicating scents and sharing thoughts. They laughed and jokingly frowned over their contrasting preferences, finding joy in the simple act of exploring scents together. Manjit's positivity to create a normal and enjoyable day had a profound effect on Sudi. She realised that even in the face of challenging circumstances, there were moments of happiness to be found. Being present with her daughter and embracing those small moments became a source of strength for both of them.

After trying several perfumes, Manjit finally found a fragrance that captured her attention. It was a delicate blend of floral and citrus notes, and she couldn't help but giggle as she sprayed it on her wrist. Sudi watched her daughter with pride and love, grateful for the opportunity to share this day with her.

As they left the fragrance shop, their spirits lifted and their bond strengthened, they continued their day with renewed energy, cherishing the time they had left together.

No matter what challenges lay ahead, Manjit and Sudi knew that they could face them together, finding some laughter in the simplest of moments, especially when time became less important.

CHAPTER 3

~AIRPORT COFFEE LOUNGE ~

Kay Adams was a friendly lady, who exhibited warmth and sincerity. With her longish brunette hair and friendly personality, she possessed a captivating allure. At the age of 33, she personified beauty and grace, but it was her kind-hearted nature that truly set her apart. Kay's devotion to her husband and son knew no bounds, and her love for them radiated in every facet of her existence. She cherished her family deeply, allowing her affection and care to permeate every aspect of her life. Kay Adams was a glowing example of sincerity and honesty, a lantern of love and compassion in a world that often seemed lacking in such virtues. She was a resident of Reading, where she shared her life with her husband Marcus and their son Arlo.

Her loving nature shined through in her role as a wife

and mother, as she prioritised creating a secure and supportive environment for her family. Her genuine and heartfelt connections were not limited to her immediate family but extended to friends and acquaintances as well.

Her husband, Marcus Adams, at the age of 40, displayed himself in a casual yet stylish ensemble consisting of grey joggers and matching hoodie. With his black hair slightly touched by hints of grey, he was a handsome man of friendly appearance.

There was a time when Marcus was a vibrant and spirited individual, radiating energy and passion in all that he pursued. His zest for life was contagious, inspiring those around him to embrace each endeavour with equal fervour. Marcus possessed an innate simplicity that endeared him to others, and his genuine kindness touched the hearts of both friends and family. He became a beloved figure in their lives, leaving an indelible mark through his incredible ability to make everyone laugh. Above all else, Marcus cherished his wife and son, finding immeasurable joy in their presence. His love for them was unconditional, and he would go to great lengths to ensure their happiness and well-being. However, tragedy struck Marcus which significantly altered the course of his and his family's lives. A devastating accident left him confined to a motor wheelchair, paralysed from the neck down, forever changing the trajectory of his existence.

As they settled in a coffee lounge area in the airport, Kay placed one coffee next to Marcus. She put a straw into his coffee cup and looked at Marcus, her eyes weary with concern.

"We can go back home. It's not too late," she suggested, hoping to ease the difficult situation they were in.

He struggled through delayed pronunciation and stuttering during the 10-15 minutes his life-giving ventilator allowed free breathing to speak with Kay. He firmly stated, "We've discussed this already. Please don't make it any harder than it already is."

Kay felt a wave of guilt wash over her as she apologised, "I'm sorry, I just..." Marcus interrupted her with certainty, "I'm not going to change my mind."

Kay trained her stern eyes at the young couple at the next table, feeling a surge of frustration and protectiveness towards her husband. She noticed the couple's discomfort, and their quick attempt to divert their eyes elsewhere. In a hushed tone, Kay leaned towards Marcus and shared her frustrations, expressing her anger with the way people stared at him. It seemed as though the sight of someone with a medical condition was unfamiliar to them. Marcus acknowledged Kay's sentiment and agreed, understanding that they shouldn't allow the ignorance of others to impact their own well-being. Kay's face softened at Marcus's encouragement. She realised that she had the power to control her own emotions and reactions. Kay worked hard at regulating her feelings by remaining strong, although this was extremely exhausting, she knew she had no other choice.

Marcus turned an empathetic gaze on Kay, understanding her anger. He wished he could reach out and gently place his hand on Kay's, to offer her reassurance and support. He hoped he could compensate for his inability to show this physically. Marcus was aware that sometimes words alone were not enough to mend emotional wounds or alleviate pain and allowed a heartwarming and sympathetic look to fill his face, hoping his eyes would let Kay know he acknowledged her feelings and that he was there for her, even if he couldn't physically show it. His eyes met with Kay's, and they felt an emotional connection that reminded them how they felt before his accident.

Kay took a deep breath, trying to let go of her annoyance. She smiled at Marcus, appreciating his strength and resilience. "I love you, Marcus."

Marcus smiled back. "I love you, too." He admired her loyalty and support. He felt compelled and content knowing he married a wonderful woman. After sipping their coffees, they both turned their attention back to the present moment, dedicated to making the most of their time together, despite the judgmental glances around them. They found encouragement in their love and support for one another, creating a bubble of warmth, enclosed from the discomfort of the outside world.

CHAPTER 4

~AIRPORT FOOD COURT~

Claire Rose, at 37 years old, exuded a unique charm that transcended societal expectations and norms. Her natural attractiveness was apparent to those who had encountered her, despite her indifference towards her appearance. She possessed an inherent beauty that emanated from within and captivated others, illustrating that true beauty which goes beyond external aesthetics.

Claire was heavier than what society considered ideal. Her weight added to her individuality but caused a subdued demeanour. In addition to her physical presence, Claire carried herself with an air of childlike innocence and naivety, as if she had yet to fully grasp the complexities of the world. Compassion flowed through Claire's veins because she possessed a deep empathy for others. However, a numbness pervaded her being, dampening her ability to fully connect with those around her. Her depression weighed heavily upon her, rendering her unable to engage in gainful employment. Emptiness and pain flooded her existence, drowning out any ray of hope or joy. Claire had faced difficult relationships, a job loss that shook her confidence, and the loss of a family member. Each blow seemed to chip away at her spirit, leaving her feeling vulnerable and alone. She found pleasure in food, using it as a way to fill the void and temporarily escape from her pain.

As time went on, Claire's relationship with food became increasingly unhealthy. She turned to it not only for comfort but as a way to punish herself for her perceived failures.

Binge-eating episodes became more frequent, leaving her feeling guilty and ashamed. The brief moments of bliss she experienced while indulging in her favourite foods were always followed by a deep sense of regret and self-loathing.

Claire's upbringing was marked by the challenges her troubled mother faced with her own pain, which had a significant impact on her ability to be a loving and nurturing parent. To make matters worse, Claire's father was an alcoholic and abandoned both of them when she was just six years old. This left Claire feeling incredibly isolated, as her mother's sadness spiralled out of control. The combination of her mother's struggles and her father's absence created a profoundly lonely environment for Claire to grow up in.

Claire's journey was one of perpetual struggle, as she wrestled with the intense depths of her emotions. Her battles with depression had left her feeling adrift in a sea of darkness. Yet, for many years, there always remained a flicker of resilience within her, a tiny flame that held the potential for rekindling her spirit. But unfortunately, over time, the light blew out and it never returned.

As she sat in the dining court area, surrounded by the flurry of travellers and the scent of freshly baked pizza, Claire found her happy place in the simple delight of indulging in her favourite comfort food and rushed to order her desired meal. The taste of the pepperoni, the warm, gooey cheese, and the savoury whiff of dough provided a temporary distraction from the turbulence within her. The fizzy Coke enlightened her senses. As Claire wiped the drips of sauce and grease from her face with a napkin, she let out a heavy sigh. The taste of the pizza and the fizz of the Coke brought a momentary sense of pleasure, but it quickly dissipated, leaving behind the familiar emptiness.

Claire left behind a tiny, scraggly flat in Crawley, West Sussex, a home where she hid from the outside world. The silent thoughts played heavily on Claire's mind as she thought about how the flat walls closed in on her, amplifying her feelings of loneliness and isolation. She yearned for human connection, for someone who could understand and share her emotions. However, her mental health struggles and subdued attitude made it challenging for her to reach out and form any meaningful relationships. The invisible barriers she had built around herself kept others at a distance, leaving her feeling trapped within the confines of her mind. The world outside felt distant and unfamiliar, as if it belonged to another reality.

Claire observed people going about their lives, seemingly connected and engaged with one another. But for her, it was an intangible realm, an existence she felt separated from.

Claire's longing for genuine connection intensified with each passing day. She wished for someone who could see beyond her closed disposition, someone who could break through the walls she had built. But the fear of rejection and the issues of her insecurities held her back, trapping her in her void of pain. Depression had stolen Claire's ability to find interest in the simplest of things. The pain she carried within her seemed insurmountable, casting a shadow over every aspect of her life. It had become a barrier that prevented her from pursuing her passions.

The journey ahead was uncertain and packed with fear, but she was determined to find a path towards healing and reclaim her life from the clutches of depression. As she stuffed her face with the remaining crumbs and fallen pepperoni, Claire's gaze drifted aimlessly around the airport, a deflated expression on her face. She took a deep breath, willing herself to push past the numbness and face her final moments. She glanced over to the newsagents, which faced the fast food area, and saw a man standing near the entrance. He appeared to be in his mid-40s, wearing a black leather jacket and jeans. His hands were stuffed in his pockets, and he seemed to be scanning the surroundings with a cautious expression on his face.

Claire noticed that he occasionally glanced at the newsagents' entrance as if he were waiting for someone or something. Intrigued by his behaviour, she decided to observe him for a little while longer to see if anything transpired.

CHAPTER 5

~THE NEWSAGENTS~

As Dave reached into his pocket to retrieve something, his grip slipped, causing his coins to spill out onto the floor. The coins scattered in different directions, creating a small commotion as they clinked against the hard surface. Dave's face flushed with embarrassment as he realised what had happened. Quickly, he crouched to the ground, hastily collecting the scattered coins. Passersby glanced in his direction. Some offered sympathetic smiles while others continued on their way, unaffected by the mishap. Dave took a deep breath, trying to appear composed despite his current predicament. He carefully gathered each coin, placing them back into his pocket one by one. As Dave bent back down to pick up his final coin, he failed to notice the middle-aged lady walking behind him. Unfortunately they both ended up colliding into one another. Dave was flustered and apologetic. He mumbled an apology to the lady, trying to gather his thoughts and make amends for his clumsiness. However, the middle-aged lady, clearly unimpressed by the incident, gave him a frowning look and brushed herself off.

"I'm sorry, ma'am. That was entirely my fault," Dave stammered, attempting to regain his composure. The lady, still wearing a displeased expression, simply nodded curtly and adjusted her belongings. Without saying a word, she walked away, leaving him feeling stupid and regretful for the accident.

Dave took another long breath, trying to acquire some self-control despite his clumsiness. With a modest smile, Dave glanced around to ensure he hadn't inconvenienced anyone. Satisfied that the area was clear, he continued on his way, making a mental note to be more mindful of his actions in the future.

CHAPTER 6

~THE FOOD COURT~

Claire's fascination with the tumult heightened, where she watched Dave who seemed to have recovered from his coin blunder and moved on. Claire's mobile rang, interrupting her observation of Dave. She glanced at the screen to see her mother's name displayed. With dread she answered the call, bringing the phone to her ear. Claire greeted her mother with worry because she hadn't discussed her plans or even explained where she was travelling to. Claire was a rubbish liar and her mother could always smell out any dishonesty.

Her mother's voice sounded concerned on the other end of the line. "What are you up to? You haven't bothered to get in touch?"

Claire took another sip of her coke, trying to find the right words, "Just had a lot on my plate lately, Mum."

Her mother responded, her tone softened a bit, "Like

what?"

"Just stuff, you know." Claire Not wanting to burden her mother with the details, suddenly changed the subject to "Are you okay, Mum?"

Her mother hesitated. "Yes, I'm fine, I guess. I've been busy with the usual chores, cleaning and sorting out things."

Claire nodded, even though her mother couldn't see her. "Sounds like the usual routine. I'm just out at the shop, Mum."

Her mother seized the opportunity, asking, "By the way, if you happen to come across thick leggings, would you mind getting me a pair? I'll give you the money."

Claire cautiously replied, "Sure, Mum. I'll keep an eye out for them." Her voice subtly trembled as she said, "I love you, Mum."

Her mother's response was filled with surprised delight. "Do you want to come round for dinner tomorrow?"

Claire considered the invitation. "Okay, I'll come."

Her mother's tone changed, "Don't put yourself out."

Claire reassured her, "No, it's fine. I'll be there."

"All right, then," her mother agreed, sounding

pleased. "See you tomorrow, Sugar. Keep your chin up."

"See you, Mum," Claire replied before the call ended. Feeling a weight of confusion and guilt, Claire took a moment to appreciate her mother's efforts in keeping in touch and showing concern for her well-being. She felt upset knowing she wouldn't be joining her mum for dinner. Taking a loud gulp of Coke, she wiped her greasy hands on a napkin. The bravery in her eyes grew stronger as she reminded herself of her goal. She couldn't let the numbness and despair control her any longer. It was time to face her final moments of familiarity and embrace the unknown that awaited her. Claire gathered her belongings and made her way towards the departure gate. The weight of her baggage, both physical and emotional, seemed to grow lighter with each step. She knew that the path she was embarking on wouldn't be easy, but she was willing to face it head-on.

As Claire zig-zagged through the airport terminal, her mind drifted back to her childhood. She wondered what life would have been like if her childhood had been different. Would she have had more opportunities? Would she have pursued different passions and interests? Would she have been happy, been in love?

These thoughts occupied her mind as she made her way through the crowded airport. With her small case in tow, she walked briskly towards the flight screen to double-check the gate and flight number. Confirming that it was indeed gate 9 for flight 21884 to Sweden, she followed the signs that directed her to the designated gate.

The airport was abuzz with passengers rushing to catch their flights, but Claire remained focused on reaching her gate on time. She weaved through the crowds, occasionally glancing at the overhead signs to ensure she was heading in the right direction. The announcement for flight 21884 to Sweden played over the speakers once again, reminding her to hurry.

CHAPTER 7

~GATE 9: FLIGHT TO SWEDEN~

Claire finally arrived at gate 9. She joined the queue of passengers waiting to board. Her eyes widened in recognition; she recognised the man standing in front of her in the queue.

It was the same person she had seen outside the newsagents who had dropped his change. A small smile tugged at the corners of her lips as the memory of that moment came rushing back.

As he nervously rummaged through his bag, emptying its contents in search of his passport, Claire observed the scene with a faint smile. She found his fumbling and nervousness endearing, appreciating his genuine effort to locate his important travel documents. While Claire initially found amusement in his momentary forgetfulness, she understood that everyone can have moments of disorganisation or distraction in situations as hectic as travelling. As such, she refrained from judgement and instead quietly shared in his relief when he finally discovered his boarding pass and passport safely tucked inside his coat pocket. With his belongings back in order, he took a loud lungful of air, visibly attempting to calm his nerves. Claire, sensing his need for reassurance, decided to offer a kind gesture.

She nervously, but teasingly, said, "Quite the scare there, huh? Almost lost your ticket to paradise."

He turned to face Claire, a delightful grin on his face. He laughed, "Yeah, you could say. Thanks for not laughing too hard."

Claire fiddled anxiously with her passport, built up the courage, and replied lightly, "Don't worry, your secret's safe with me."

Dave blushed. They exchanged a friendly glance, and the tension in the air eased. Dave noticed a middle-aged man manoeuvring his motorised wheelchair towards the front of the queue. Dave showed a lack of etiquette by carefully observing Marcus breathing via the ventilator attached to his mouth from his neck. Dave's stare was full of empathy but lacked common sense. He almost forgot to make room for the man. Dave apologised and moved to one side almost causing another collision with the man's wife, who was carrying two small cases of luggage.

At the back of the same queue, Manjit and her mum hurriedly joined, feeling relieved that they had made it in time. As they settled into their place, they took a moment to catch their breath and appreciate their accomplishment. The queue seemed to stretch endlessly in front of them, lined with people patiently waiting.

Manjit pressed her mum's shoulder affectionately, expressing her relief. "I told you we'd make it."

Sudi returned the smile unconvincingly, "Only just. I'm just glad you made up your mind about the perfume."

Manjit grinned with pride, "Well, at least I smell damn good."

The queue gradually moved forward, and they inched closer to the gate. Other people around them were chatting, reading books, looking at their mobiles, or lost in their own thoughts.

Finally, after what felt like an eternity, it was nearly their turn. There was a long silence between Manjit and Sudi. Sudi worriedly looked at Manjit. Reluctant to share her thoughts, she gently and carefully opened up, "There was a moment back there, I thought you deliberately wanted to miss the flight?"

This made Manjit feel upset and guilty, unsure how to respond. She quietly replied, "No."

Sudi was desperate for Manjit to change her mind. Knowing she had previously angered Manjit with her persistence she wanted to give this one last shot, but worried how Manjit would react, she bravely said, "We can always turn back, you know?"

Manjit understood her mum's attempts. She didn't want to upset her mum any further, so with sadness, she calmly looked at Sudi, "If only it were that simple."

Not exactly the words Sudi wanted to hear, however, she did feel at ease by the fact she tried and that it

didn't cause any unwanted discomfort. Sudi gently held Manjit's hand. She and Manjit stepped forward with a mixture of fear and uncertainty to experience whatever awaited them. They exchanged one last glance, sharing a silent understanding of why they were there. They both presented their boarding passes to the airline staff who scanned them and allowed them to proceed. With a sense of relief they stepped onto the jet bridge, ready to embark on their journey to Sweden.

CHAPTER 8

~SWEDEN~

The airport was filled with a sense of urgency and excitement, with people from all walks of life. Passengers were seen rushing through the crowds, pulling their suitcases behind them as they searched for the exits. The sound of rolling wheels and the occasional clatter of bags hitting the ground could be heard throughout the terminal.

As Dave stepped outside the airport, he took a moment to indulge in a cigarette. The noisy atmosphere of the airport was replaced by a slightly calmer environment, although there were still people coming and going, taxis lined up, and the occasional sound of car horns. Dave found a spot away from the main entrance, ensuring that he was in a designated smoking area.

He took out his lighter, flicked it open, and ignited the end of his cigarette. As he inhaled, a sense of temporary relaxation flowed over him. He looked around, watching the comings and goings of people outside the airport. Some were eagerly hailing taxis, while others were bidding farewell to loved ones or waiting for rides. The atmosphere buzzed like a live wire with a sense of anticipation, as if each person were a charged particle waiting to collide. A fresh start and new beginnings, like a garden ready to burst into bloom after a long winter.

As Dave observed from a distance, he recognised the woman from the flight queue. A sense of happiness grew around him as he realised that he knew her. He stayed focused on her as she effortlessly balanced eating her burger with pulling her suitcase along. He noticed her skillfully cruising through the people who wandered back and forth outside. She seemed focused and determined, yet there was a hint of relaxation and contentment on her face as she enjoyed her meal.

Dave's imagination started to unfold, wondering where she might be heading and what adventures awaited her. He contemplated approaching her but felt that would create an awkward situation. So he decided to observe her from afar. He watched as she made her way towards the taxi rank, her suitcase rolling smoothly behind her. It appeared that she was ready to continue her journey beyond the airport. Dave couldn't help thinking if they might be heading in the same direction or if their paths would diverge.

Dave sniggered with cynicism, shaking his head in reaction to his delusional thoughts. The cigarette slowly burnt down, and he stubbed it out, discarding it in a nearby ashtray. He exhaled a puff of smoke, feeling a sense of clarity. He had made his decision and there was no going back.

CHAPTER 9

~SWEDISH TAXI RIDE~

Manjit and Sudi sat side by side on the backseat of a taxi, their eyes fixed on the breathtaking panorama of the Swedish Mountains that stretched out before them. The hills, blanketed in lush greenery and sparkling with pristine snow, painted a picture of unparalleled beauty. As the taxi wound its way through the curving roads, Sudi couldn't help but be captivated by the sheer magnificence of their surroundings. The sunlight danced on the snowy peaks, casting an ethereal radiance that seemed to set the entire landscape aglow. It was a scene straight out of a postcard, one that took their breath away. Manjit, sitting beside her with the car door window half open, breathed in the crisp mountain air with a sense of awe. Her eyes sparkled with delight as she absorbed the splendour of nature's masterpiece. The serenity of the mountains provided a welcome respite from the difficulties they faced. Sudi desperately needed a distraction from this present journey and from the turmoil back home in Fulham, London, where she lived with her husband.

Sudi was happily married to Dhruv, Manjit's father. They had three other children, all young men. Dhruv was an individual rooted in the traditions of his Indian heritage, embodying an old-fashioned manner. He held immense value for his family's customs and practices, cherished their importance in his life.

Although he harboured deep love for his family, Dhruv's affectionate nature was sometimes hidden by his reserved and quiet manner. A deeply religious person, Dhruv found comfort in his faith and diligently followed its teachings. He was known for his strong work ethic, dedicating himself wholeheartedly to his professional endeavours. He had always set high expectations for himself and those around him, always striving for excellence in all aspects of life.

They had gotten married when they were 17, and their relationship had always been tight. However, their current situation caused tremendous heartbreak and tension. Sudi and Manjit planned their trip to Sweden, but Dhruv was completely against it. He refused to engage in any conversation about the trip, which had caused a significant upset within their large, close-knit family.

Despite their generally happy marriage, the disagreement over the trip had created a rift between Sudi and her husband. It seemed that he had strong reservations and concerns about the ethics of it and how this tragic event would impact them, but he hadn't expressed them openly or even engaged in a productive discussion with Sudi or Manjit. This lack of communication led to frustration and disappointment, not only for Sudi and Manjit but also for other family members who witnessed the conflict. The family were confused and concerned about Manjit's decision. They also questioned Sudi's motives in supporting her. They were worried about the tension between Sudi and her husband as it went against the harmony they had always enjoyed.

In the meantime, Sudi had been left feeling torn between her daughter's wishes to go on the trip and her commitment to her husband. She understood the importance of open communication and compromise in a marriage, but she also yearned to be there for her daughter.

The taxi driver, sensing their admiration for the landscape, occasionally pointed out notable landmarks and shared stories of the region. Manjit and Sudi listened attentively, their hearts filled with appreciation for the unique experience they were having. It was as if the mountains whispered tales of resilience and endurance, inspiring them to face their challenges with renewed strength. As the taxi continued its journey, the green and snow-covered hills seemed to change with each passing mile. The scenery morphed from gentle slopes to towering peaks, from dense forests to open meadows. Every twist and turn revealed a new facet of nature's grandeur, leaving Sudi and Manjit in a state of constant wonder. In that shared moment, surrounded by the majesty of the Swedish Mountains, Sudi and Manjit renewed a sense of connection.

They realised that no matter how difficult their circumstances, the beauty of the world would always be there.

As the taxi approached their destination, Manjit and Sudi exchanged a knowing glance. The memory of this journey would forever be carved in their hearts, a reminder of the power of nature to heal and uplift. They stepped out of the taxi, their souls nourished by the beauty they had witnessed. Manjit and Sudi's eyes were immediately drawn to the white, clean, beautiful building in front of them. The architecture exhibited an abundance of elegance and charm, perfectly complementing the surrounding scenery. The building stood as a testament to meticulous design and attention to detail.

As they took in the view, a sense of doubt washed over them. The manicured gardens and vibrant flowers added a touch of natural beauty to the already picturesque scene. The gentle breeze was loaded with the scents of nature and a sense of tranquillity. The taxi driver, aware of the importance of their luggage, handled it with care, gingerly placing it on the ground. He ensured that their belongings were safely unloaded, taking his time to make sure nothing was damaged. His professionalism and attention to detail reflected the high level of service they would expect in this serene environment.

Manjit and Sudi exchanged doubtful glances, their

expressions reflected how anxiously they waited to explore and immerse themselves in the dazzling serenity of their surroundings. As they stepped forward, the entrance of the building beckoned them with its charm. They walked towards it, encapsulated in pain and sorrow. Sudi looked at her daughter.

"Are you okay?" she asked, noticing the agitation in Manjit's appearance.

Manjit sighed softly. "I'm a bit nervous and in pain," her voice trembled slightly at her admission.

Sudi understood and nodded in response, offering a comforting smile. "Let's get you settled, my dear. I'll be here when you wake up," she assured her daughter.

Sudi reached out and placed a comforting hand on Manjit's arm, inquiring if she had taken her medication. Manjit affirmed that she had, acknowledging that it provided some relief by taking the edge off. Grateful for the small respite it offered, she appreciated her mother's concern. Sudi, in turn, couldn't help but admire her daughter's elegance, expressing pride in her appearance and complimenting her beauty.

Manjit blushed at the praise, a mix of embarrassment and warmth flooding her emotions. She attempted to deflect the attention by protesting her mother's compliments. Sudi's expression turned thoughtful as she voiced her curiosity about Manjit's choice not to settle down despite having the opportunity to be with anyone.

Pondering her mother's words, Manjit gazed back at her, a hint of longing in her voice as she explained that maybe she hadn't wanted just anyone. This statement left Sudi puzzled, prompting her to question Manjit further to understand her perspective.

Struggling to articulate her feelings, Manjit admitted that it hadn't been easy in a voice tinged with sadness. Sudi sought clarification, asking what exactly had been difficult for her daughter. Manjit, feeling a sense of resignation, decided it was futile to delve further into the matter, expressing that it wouldn't be comprehensible to her mother and that discussing it now wouldn't serve any purpose. Realising that some things were beyond her mother's understanding, Manjit chose to leave the topic untouched.

Sudi found herself grappling with a confusing blend of frustration and uncertainty, openly acknowledging her bewilderment. In an earnest effort to mend the emotional gap that had widened between them, she endeavoured to bridge the divide that had emerged. Meanwhile, Manjit averted her gaze and directed her attention towards the picturesque surroundings, remarking on the beauty in an attempt to shift the focus and find peace in the tranquillity of the moment. Sudi followed suit, admiring the breathtaking scenery and momentarily losing herself in the natural splendour that surrounded them.

As Manjit's exhaustion became palpable, her drooping eyes and fatigued voice betrayed her weariness. She expressed her fatigue to her mother, confessing her need for rest. Sudi, guided by her maternal instinct, gently brushed a strand of hair away from Manjit's face as she inquired with sensitivity about her well-being. Manjit weakly nodded, acknowledging her need for a nap to recharge. Understanding her daughter's fatigue, Sudi responded with a nod, offering a reassuring smile as she suggested getting Manjit settled in for some rest. Again assuring her daughter that she would be there when she woke up, Sudi provided comfort and support in that moment of vulnerability.

CHAPTER 10

~THE CLINIC~

Manjit and Sudi entered into the clinic's immaculate reception area and were immediately captivated by its grandeur. Their eyes were drawn to an angelic fountain, its cascading water created a soothing and serene ambiance. The gentle sound of the water added a touch of equanimity to the environment, which invited a sense of calmness to those who entered.

As they approached the reception desk, they were greeted by a friendly receptionist who maintained the same level of elegance and professionalism that permeated the entire area. "Hello and welcome," the receptionist said cheerfully, as she glanced down at her list, "You must be Manjit, and this is your mum, Sudi?"

Manjit nodded, her nerves evident in her slight fidgeting. "Yes, that's right. We are expected today at 3 pm," she replied, her voice crackling with anticipation and anxiety.

The receptionist extended her hand towards them, "Lovely to meet you both, please take a seat in the lounge area." She gestured towards a comfortable seating arrangement nearby. The warm and welcoming conduct of the receptionist added a personal touch to the gloriousness of the space, making Manjit and Sudi feel relaxed and cared for.

"Thanks," Manjit said, her gratitude noticeable in her tone. She appreciated the receptionist's friendly presence, which helped to ease her nerves.

The lounge was designed for comfort, embellished with designer seating, soft lighting, and serene decor. The atmosphere induced a sense of calmness, providing a sanctuary for those in need of quiet reflection. Manjit and Sudi followed the receptionist's guidance and settled into plush chairs. They positioned themselves close together, finding comfort in each other's presence. Sudi reached out and gently squeezed her daughter's hand in silent support. They noticed a couple, Kay and Marcus, sitting opposite them. Sudi greeted them with a warm smile as they looked over at them. It was a chance encounter, and the air hung with a sense of unfamiliarity.

"Hello," Sudi said with genuine warmth. Kay returned the greeting, her voice friendly but tinged with a hint of reservation. Kay responded with a simple "Hello" in return, and an uncomfortable pause settled between them. The silence was broken as Kay attempted to bridge the gap and initiate a conversation.

"Where have you travelled from?" Kay asked a bit curiously.

Manjit, sitting quietly beside her mother, spoke up, "England, Stansted."

A spark of recognition flickered in Kay's eyes. "We caught a flight from Stansted, I bet we were on the same one?" she wondered, a touch of excitement creeping into her voice. Manjit nodded, her weariness palpable. She glanced over at Sudi, silently conveying her fatigue. Sudi understood her daughter's unspoken plea for support and placed a comforting hand on Manjit's arm.

Kay's compassion was obvious as she comforted Marcus, who appeared visibly worried and anxious as he sat quietly in his motorised chair, breathing into his ventilator.

Manjit and Sudi observed the exchange, and they

recognised the shared emotions of concern and unease.

There was a loud bang from the entrance door. Startled by the sudden noise, their heads turned towards the main entrance where the sound reverberated through the room. Curious eyes shifted in the direction of the disturbance. Sudi and Marcus were sitting opposite each other, they exchanged glances, their inquisitive minds aroused by the unexpected sound. Their eyes reflected surprise and concern. It was unclear what the startling sound was so they instinctively leaned closer together, seeking reassurance in each other's presence. Kay, with an edge of nervousness, looked towards the entrance to investigate the cause of the noise. Marcus' eyes followed closely behind, a protective instinct guiding his thoughts.

As they observed the door, they discovered that it had been opened forcefully by a young woman with her wheeled suitcase. Leaves swirled in the air outside, carried by the sudden breeze. Relief washed over them, realising that there was no immediate danger. They traded looks, amusement, and relief on their faces. The initial tension and unfamiliarity seemed to dissipate, replaced by a shared moment of light-heartedness. Sudi, Manjit, Marcus, and Kay shared a smile, a connection formed in that unexpected moment. It was as if the sound had broken the barriers between them, allowing them to see one another in a different light.

As Claire struggled to free her suitcase from between the doors, frustration and anger welled up inside her. With sheer force she managed to yank it free, the noise continued to echo throughout the entrance and vibrated through the other end of the building. Without wasting a moment, she marched straight towards the reception desk, her emotions noticeable in her body language and defensive stride.

The receptionist at the front desk greeted Claire with a warm smile as she entered the building. "Hello, welcome. You must be Claire Rose?" the receptionist asked.

Claire affirmed, "Yes, that's me."

The receptionist extended her hand. "Lovely to meet you," she added, "Please take a seat in the lounge area, and someone will be with you shortly."

"Thanks," Claire approved, making her way to the comfortable seating area. Just as Claire approached the lounge area, another person walked through the entrance. It was the man who had met Claire earlier at the airport. Claire smiled, recognising him from their encounter. The receptionist turned her attention to Dave.

"Hello, Sir. Welcome. You must be Dave Wilson?" she asked.

Dave's eyes were spell-bound with surprise and shock as he caught sight of Claire. He was completely taken aback by her presence and found himself staring at her, momentarily forgetting his name.

"Mr. Wilson?" the receptionist repeated, trying to bring Dave back to the conversation.

Dave snapped out of his daze and quickly regained his focus. "Err, sorry. I'm Dave," he managed to share, feeling a bit flustered.

Claire joined the others in the lounge area. Their worries lingered between them, which created a bond of uncertainty. Dave approached the group with an awkward stroll, oblivious to the red sauce smeared on his chin. While everyone noticed the conspicuous stain, a nonverbal decision was made to refrain from mentioning it, perhaps out of kindness or to avoid potential embarrassment. The unspoken agreement amused Claire, who found pleasant relief in the others' camaraderie.

When Dave settled down next to Claire, his presence brought a sense of encouragement. They glanced at each other, their eyes met briefly, conveying a shared understanding and silent acknowledgment of their connection. Claire's half-smile widened slightly, a sign of her genuine pleasure at seeing Dave.

He built up the courage to break the awkwardness, "Fancy seeing you here?"

Claire smirked stupidly, unsure how to respond. Saving them from entering into a weird conversation a sudden sharp sound pierced the silence, an unmistakable tap-tap-tapping of high heels. The noise grew louder, drawing nearer with each rhythmic step. The taps symbolised confidence and power.

With an air of authority and self-assurance, a lady strode purposefully towards the group. Her ID badge swung from side to side, displaying her authority and professional role. She was dressed in a crisp white medical gown that accentuated her seriousness and purpose. Michelle Reynolds, aged 56, was a slim lady with mid-length dyed blonde hair. Her hair showed signs of ageing, with some grey roots starting to show through the dyed colour. She wore a noticeable amount of makeup which included heavy foundation, bright eyeshadow, and bold lipstick. The makeup gave her a somewhat artificial appearance, which possibly indicated a desire to project a certain image or to boost her confidence.

Michelle's persona was characterised by an overconfident attitude, which made it difficult to gauge her true intentions or emotions. She came across as assertive and self-assured, but there might have been an underlying insecurity or a need to compensate for something.

Despite this, Michelle's professional role and authority were still evident through her ID and the way she carried herself. While her appearance and behaviour might raise some questions, there could be more to Michelle's story than met the eye.

As she walked closer to the group, her presence commanded attention. Clutching a file of papers firmly in her hands, Michelle showed her preparedness and attention to detail. Her firm grip on the file suggested that she valued organisation and precision in her work. The file itself represented her knowledge and expertise, containing important information that she was possibly prepared to present or discuss with the group.

As she proceeded nearer, the others couldn't help noticing her bold, striking lipstick. Disapproval was obvious in the eyes of Sudi, Marcus and Manjit. The side-long glances indicated a collective similarity in what they deemed as too much, believing a woman of her age should conform to more muted tones.

CHAPTER 11

~THE TOUR~

Michelle greeted the group with a nod, welcoming them with a positive vibe as she initiated the interaction. Leading with a rhetorical question, she inquired about the smoothness of their journey, prompting the group to respond with nods and murmured greetings, fascinated by Michelle's presence. With a disdainful glance at her file, Michelle shifted towards a more formal tone as she went about confirming the attendees.

Manjit, Dave, and Claire reluctantly raised their hands in acknowledgment. Turning to Kay, Michelle queried about her identity, to which Kay pointed to her husband, Marcus, validating his presence by introducing him. Michelle acknowledged Marcus with a murmured greeting before shifting her gaze to Manjit, offering a quick half-smile as she greeted her. Manjit, feeling agitated at the assumption and association of her name with the colour of her skin, simply responded with a brief "Hi."

Michelle then directed her attention to Claire, who introduced herself gently as she exchanged greetings. Without seeking confirmation, Michelle identified Dave and engaged him, noticing his distraction and slight confusion. Dave eventually confirmed his identity as Dave Wilson, responding to Michelle's inquiry. Concluding the introductions, Michelle expressed her pleasure at meeting the group, introducing herself as the manager and assuring them that she would soon get them settled in. Before proceeding, she mentioned her intention to give them a tour of the visitors' area.

Dave interjected, seeking clarification about the timing of an event scheduled for the next day. Michelle reassured the group that they could ask for a reminder of the schedule if needed. Kay and Manjit confirmed they had copies of the schedule for the following day. Michelle acknowledged their readiness and informed them that each of their rooms would also have a copy of the schedule. Signalling for them to follow her, she instructed the group to proceed.

Feeling a hint of nervousness, Dave turned to Claire before they moved, expressing anticipation. Claire noticed something on Dave's chin and subtly pointed it out to him, suggesting he check his chin. Puzzled, Dave rubbed his chin, his cheeks flushing with patches of red as he searched for the blemish.

Michelle led the group through the facility, providing them with a tour. Pausing to address the group, she pointed out the dining area and began walking towards it. Kay, intrigued by another area to the right, inquired about its purpose, noting the double set of black doors marked 'NO ENTRY'.

Responding sharply to the interruption, Michelle clarified that the area was restricted before resuming her explanation about the dining area. She described the refreshments and snacks available for purchase, including a menu with hot and cold beverages like coffee, tea, soft drinks, and juices, as well as snacks such as sandwiches, pastries, and fruit cups. Michelle paused briefly, allowing the group to absorb the information before continuing with the tour.

Michelle proceeded to inform the group about the outdoor sitting area where they could relax and enjoy their refreshments after making their purchases. She described the space as located at the back of the building, featuring comfortable seating and a pleasant ambiance. Michelle's warm smile conveyed her enthusiasm as she highlighted the enchanting nature of the outdoor sitting area, particularly in the evening when it was illuminated with beautiful lights. She reassured the group about any concerns regarding the weather by mentioning the presence of outdoor heaters to ensure their comfort in case it became too chilly.

As they approached the dining area, there stood a communal restaurant called 'Harmony Haven'. It was a place where visitors and family could gather, seeking distraction and companionship over a warm meal. Yet on this evening, the restaurant wore a cloak of bleak stillness. As the quiet afternoon painted the sky in shades of violet and gold, the earlier bustling establishment appeared deserted. The soft glow of modern lanterns spilled their warm light onto polished white glossy tables adorned with pristine white chairs. A delicate melody of hushed whispers, as if the space held its breath waiting for life to return, wafted through the air, mingled with the faint scent of cinnamon that lingered from the morning's baking. The sound of a ticking clock echoed gently, marking the passage of time in measured beats. Sunlight filtered through the lacey curtains, casting intricate patterns on the clean wooden floors, but there were no footsteps to disturb its dance.

The chairs neatly arranged around the tables, sat in anticipation, their welcoming arms empty and untouched. The walls, decorated with abstract paintings depicting lively scenes of laughter and companionship, seemed to long for the voices that once animated those very moments. Behind the polished counter, the barista's station stood silent, the gleaming espresso machine dormant, its steaming wand poised in mid-air as if frozen in time. The shelves that once held an array of savoury pastries and delectable treats now showcased empty spaces, waiting to be filled with culinary delights.

Through the large windows, the outside world whispered its secrets. Leaves rustled in the gentle breeze and a distant bird sang its melancholic tune. But within the walls of Harmony Haven, the silence reigned supreme, as if the world had decided to pause for a moment, allowing the restaurant to catch its breath. The stillness held a certain beauty—a serene emptiness that offered a canvas for imagination. It was a place where stories could be woven, memories could be shaped, and deep voices in conversation lingered in the air. Though the restaurant stood empty and quiet, its heartbeat with anticipation of the next gathering, the next feast of shared experiences.

Harmony Haven was not merely a physical space, it was an emblem of the clinic. A haven where people would gather once more, filling the silence with their thoughts and precious moments. And until that time, it patiently waited, embracing the sedation of the present, knowing that its purpose would be fulfilled again.

Stepping through the doors, a sense of warmth wrapped them. The area was thoughtfully enhanced with five sturdy picnic benches arranged in a circle, encouraging conversation to flow freely. Each bench was meticulously crafted from polished wood, providing a comfortable place to sit and unwind. To combat the chill of the evening breeze, a row of elegant heaters, as Michelle mentioned, stood tall along the perimeter of the sitting area. Their dim glow cast a soft light, adding a touch of enchantment to the space. The heaters hummed gently, creating a warm restful atmosphere to embrace visitors who craved a reflective moment. The focal point of the communal area was the meticulously manicured lawn. A vibrant oasis of green amid the landscape, the soft grass invited people to kick off their shoes and revel in the simple pleasure of nature's touch. Surrounding the entire space a sturdy fence, six feet in height, provided a shield from the outside world. It acted as a guardian protecting the tranquillity within from the chaos beyond. The fence, painted in a neutral hue, blended seamlessly with its surroundings, allowing the communal area to exist as a quiet sanctuary amidst the outside noise of life. Day or night, the communal outside sitting area released a sense of unity and belonging. It was a haven for those seeking a quiet escape, a place to indulge in one's own thoughts, and the calming ritual of smoking. Here within the entrapment of the fence, under the watchful gaze of the heaters, strangers became friends and the outside world faded into the background.

Michelle led the group back inside and closed the door behind her. She gestured towards the dining area as she formally addressed the group. "When you get settled in, feel free to explore or simply enjoy the atmosphere. Maybe grab something to eat or drink from the vending machine?" Just as Michelle finished speaking, her walkie-talkie emitted a sound, indicating an incoming message.

A voice from the walkie-talkie called out urgently, "We need some assistance at Bay 1.

Michelle quickly picked up her walkie-talkie and responded, "Copy that. I'm on my way." She turned to the group, apologising. "Sorry about this, it shouldn't take long. Please feel free to buy refreshments." With that, she hurried off towards the restricted area, leaving the group confused. As the group stood there, Michelle's sudden departure created an awkward scene, leaving them all perplexed.

Manjit, always one to speak her mind, broke the silence by expressing her thoughts. "Well, that was weird," her eyes followed Michelle's retreating figure.

Kay turned to Marcus, sensing his disinterest in the situation. "Would you like anything?" She tried offering some distraction. Marcus shook his head, declining her offer.

"No, thanks," his attention was still fixed on his surroundings.

Manjit, eager to engage in conversation, turned her

attention to Claire and Dave. "Are you two together?" she inquired, her curiosity getting the better of her.

Claire and Dave both shook their heads with embarrassment. "No," they answered in unison.

Manjit, wanting to keep the conversation flowing, remarked on the uncomfortable atmosphere. "Feels surreal being here, doesn't it?" she voiced, her eyes scanning the surroundings.

Dave agreed.

Claire added her feelings. "Not half. I just want it over with," she claimed, her voice glitzed with weariness.

Manjit, pretending to be oblivious to the sensitive nature of her questioning, ventured further into personal territory, "Are you both terminally ill? Sorry, it's none of my business."

Clare glared at Manjit, knowing full well she wasn't sorry. She instinctively sensed that Manjit wanted to find out why they were there.

Dave, taken aback by the directness of the question, mustered the courage to answer honestly. "Depression," his voice conveyed both vulnerability and strength.

Claire, feeling a connection with Dave's admission, chipped in, "Yeah, me too." Their eyes met, filled with understanding and shared experiences.

Manjit, bewildered and surprised by their responses, struggled to comprehend. "I didn't realise people could come here unless they've got a terminal or degenerative condition?" she blurted, her confusion apparent.

Sudi, uncomfortable with Manjit's probing questions, remained silent. Instead, she observed the unfolding conversation, trying to make sense of the diverse perspectives and emotions in the group.

Kay initiated conversation with Sudi, providing a welcome distraction from the intense exchange. Suddenly, Claire anxiously but firmly defended herself by informing Manjit that there had been a change in the law that permitted individuals, including people with serious mental health disorders, to travel to legal euthanasia clinics with their doctor's support.

Manjit, visibly emotional, requested clarification about Claire's physical well-being causing Dave and Claire to become uncomfortable. Sudi noticed the tension, so she decided to address

Manjit who was now upset and voicing her frustration aloud, strongly expressed her belief that they were both fit and well, but that she didn't have the option to live. Sudi gently pulled Manjit away from Dave and Claire.

During the confrontational conversation Michelle suddenly reappeared, breaking the tense atmosphere and offered an apology for her sudden departure.

"Sorry about that," she said, with a lack of sincerity and then requested the group to continue following her, "Right, let's head this way." Michelle quickly marched forward, leaving the others to catch up. She pointed towards the left side of the building, signalling the group to follow her closely. The others rushed behind her, their anticipation increasing with each step. They passed through a set of double doors on the ground floor as Michelle continued to guide them through the unfamiliar surroundings.

As their tour continued, Manjit turned to her mother, feeling another wave of exhaustion. Sensing her daughter's fatigue, Sudi nodded, "I think you need some rest," she acknowledged, her concern clear in her voice.

"Nearly to your rooms, dear," Michelle overheard their conversation, so she immediately stepped in to offer reassurance. She was trying to assure Manjit so she would be silent and not interrupt further with her moaning whilst she showed them around. She led the group further down the corridor, their destination now within reach.

Guiding their attention to the left, Michelle pointed towards a doorway, "On your left is the communal kitchen," she revealed. The group took in the sight of the inviting kitchen, a sense of familiarity in the unknown. The smell of coffee filled the air, which offered a sense of comfort.

The kitchen was filled with colourful, hand-painted tiles, depicting scenes of nature and culinary delights, adding a touch of artistic charm to the space. Soft, warm lighting bathed the room, creating a warm space. To the left of the entrance stood a row of artfully mismatched chairs with a glass table. The table was decorated with a vase of wildflowers, lending a touch of natural beauty to the space. The walls had a couple of shelves lined with books of various genres, which offered visitors the opportunity to get lost in captivating stories as they savoured their culinary creations. The rear of the kitchen boasted gleaming stainless-steel countertops, assorted high-quality cooking utensils, and state-of-the-art appliances. Michelle continued guiding them.

Dave good-humouredly asked, "Where's the bar?"

Michelle, unamused and certainly not willing to engage in stupid humour, stated matter-of-factly, "No bar, I'm afraid. But you were welcome to bring your own alcohol!"

Claire caught Dave's stare and sniggered at his question. Manjit noticed their interaction and gave them a disapproving glare before sighing. Dave and Claire recognised Manjit's disapproval and exchanged a glance before they all entered another set of double doors as they continued their journey through the facility.

Michelle gestured towards a room on the right. "Here on your right, is the communal living area," her voice suddenly carried a touch of bizarre excitement. "It has a Sky TV so you can relax and unwind during your stay."

The seating option included a deluxe sofa and a couple of armchairs, which gave ample space for a small group of people to gather where they could enjoy watching TV. The furniture was arranged so everyone had a clear view of the screen and created an inclusive atmosphere. The centrepiece of the space was the flat-screen TV mounted on the wall to provide a focal point for the room.

Michelle led the group to their accommodations further down the corridor. She turned to them and confirmed, "Here are your rooms. You all have your fob keys with your numbers on, correct?"

Kay nodded, holding up her fob key. "Yep."

"Lovely. I'll let you all get settled in. My assistant will bring each of you to see me soon for a protocol assessment. It won't take long, and there's nothing to worry about. If you have any questions, please dial #1 on the phones in your room. We hope to make your stay as pleasant as possible." Kay, Sudi, Dave, and Claire prepared their fob keys with their respective room numbers.

The others smiled with reluctance; they were apprehensive about their situation.

Michelle bid them farewell. "Try and get some rest. See you shortly."

The group entered their individual rooms, numbered 1-4, which were conveniently situated next to one another. Each room was a small, cosy space designed with simplicity and cleanliness in mind. Soft, neutral tones coloured the walls creating a serene setting that welcomed travellers. Natural light would stream in through the curtained window that cast a warm glow across the room during the day.

Against one wall stood two single beds, each neatly made with crisp, white linens. The mattresses were firm and inviting, promising a restful night's sleep after a long day. A plump pillow rested at the head of each bed, ready to cradle tired heads and offer comfort.

Between the beds, a small wooden nightstand held a sleek alarm clock and a reading lamp. The lamp emitted a gentle warm light, perfect for winding down with a good book before drifting off to sleep. A modest artwork embellished the wall above the nightstand, adding a touch of character to the otherwise minimalist room.

On the opposite wall was a well-lit practical desk boasting a comfortable chair with a convenient power outlet. Made of smoothly polished wood, it accommodated all the required items for making and enjoying tea or coffee. There was a modern stainless-steel kettle beside a collection of glass cups that varied in sizes and designs on a stand. Near the cups was a vast selection of coffee, beans or ground, and tea, in bags or loose leaves, preserved in airtight containers. Everything was labelled for quick use. There was a small organiser holding assorted sweeteners, spoons and stir sticks, and a small container for storing milk.

A compact wardrobe nestled in the corner of the room offered ample storage space for clothes and personal belongings. It featured hangers for neatly organising outfits and a small safe for guests to secure their valuables. The en-suite bathroom, though small, boasted sparkling cleanliness. It was equipped with a modern, glass-enclosed shower, a pristine sink with a polished chrome faucet, and a gleaming mirror that reflected the room's natural light, enhancing the sense of space.

Overall, the rooms exuded an air of simplicity and tidiness. While it lacked elaborate decorations or extravagant luxuries, its attention to cleanliness and practicality provided a comfortable haven for clients seeking a peaceful night's rest.

Manjit wasted no time and climbed onto her bed. She sat upright on the bed before finally dropping back onto her pillow with a sigh of relief.

"Finally," she exclaimed.

Sudi, standing nearby, encouraged her, "Get some

sleep, darling."

Just as Manjit started to relax, her mobile phone began to ring, which frightened her. Manjit yelled in frustration. She glanced at her phone and noticed she had five missed calls from Sarah. Sudi glanced over and saw the missed calls. Without saying a word, Manjit switched off her phone; she didn't have the energy to talk to anyone.

Sudi, curious why Sarah kept calling, asked, "Does she know where you are?" Ignoring the question, Manjit rolled over and prepared herself to go to sleep, signalling that she didn't want to discuss Sarah any further.

In Marcus's room, Kay held a straw. She was helping Marcus drink his beverage when her mobile phone rang, and she saw that Arlo was calling. She answered the phone, "Hello, son. Are you okay?"

Marcus, reclined in his motor chair, called out to Kay, "Say I said hello, and I love him."

Kay relayed the message to Arlo over and waited for his response. After a brief pause, she continued the conversation, "Yes, it's lovely here. Okay, babe. Yeah, we'll see you in a couple of days. Bye. Love you." She hung up the phone and placed it down, feeling guilty about lying to Arlo. She expressed her concerns to Marcus, "I hate lying to him. God knows how he's going to take it when I go back without you."

Marcus simply requested, "TV, please."

Kay turned on the television and tuned it to the news channel. She worriedly asked Marcus again, "Are you sure you don't want to talk to him? Give him an explanation? Say goodbye even?"

Marcus, resolute in his decision, responded, "No. Just tell him I'm sorry."

In a corner of Claire's room, a comfortable armchair faced a small television mounted on the wall. It served as a source of entertainment and distraction during moments of solitude. Tonight, however, Claire had chosen to turn off the television; she preferred to focus on her last thoughts.

Claire unpacked her pyjamas, toiletries, and two sets of clothes which indicated she surprisingly wanted some order. Suddenly, there was a knock at her door. She pulled open the door and found Dave standing there.

"Hey! I hope you don't mind me knocking. I just wanted to check if you were okay after what that woman, Manjit, said earlier?"

Claire reassured him, "Yeah. Do you want to come in? Have a drink?"

Dave gladly accepted the invitation and followed her into her room.

Inside the room, the layout was simple and familiar, creating a comfortable environment for Claire and Dave. Dave's attention was drawn to a bottle of vodka, a bottle of Coke, and some plastic cups neatly arranged on Claire's side table. Taking a seat on a nearby chair, he observed as she began to pour the drinks, signalling a shift in the atmosphere. Despite her usual avoidance of alcohol due to her medication, Claire felt a desire to indulge in a drink on this particular occasion. With a touch of rebellion, she declared, "I don't normally drink because of my meds, but fuck it, hey! Last night."

Embracing Claire's spontaneous decision, Dave echoed her sentiment, suggesting they might as well enjoy themselves. Claire handed Dave his drink, encouraging him to start drinking. He gratefully received the glass, taking a large sip before acknowledging the situation. Reflecting on the earlier encounter with Manjit, Dave remarked on her rudeness, prompting a shared moment of judgement towards her behaviour.

Claire attributed Manjit's demeanour to her emotional state, highlighting the complexities of living with severe depression and the challenges of being understood by others who haven't experienced it firsthand.

As they delved deeper into their conversation, Claire and Dave found solace in their shared struggles with mental health. They discussed the limitations of medication and therapy in alleviating the burdens of depression, expressing a longing for moments of happiness amidst their daily struggles. Claire's swift consumption of her vodka signalled a sense of liberation in the moment, prompting her to offer Dave another drink. Responding to her offer, Dave, with a half-full glass in hand, accepted the gesture, indicating a willingness to continue their candid conversation over another round.

It was now early evening, and Sudi sat comfortably on a chair engrossed in her book while Manjit was asleep. Suddenly, a knock at the door stirred Manjit from her sleep. Sudi hurried to open the door and was greeted by the friendly receptionist. Hi, my name is Chloe. I've come to escort Manjit for her assessment."

Sudi recognised her from reception and responded,

"Ah, yes. One minute."

Sudi stepped aside to allow Chloe to enter the room. She quickly went over to Manjit and gently shook her shoulder. "Manjit, Chloe is here to escort you for your assessment."

Manjit groggily and gradually woke up. She rubbed her eyes and nodded in understanding. Sudi and Chloe exchanged a brief smile, and Sudi moved aside to let Chloe take the lead. Chloe extended her arm and gestured for Manjit to follow her.

Manjit slowly got up from the bed to stand on wobbly legs. She glanced back at Sudi, who offered her a reassuring smile. Manjit managed a weak smile before she turned away to walk with Chloe out of the room.

Sudi watched them leave, expression full of concern and worry. She closed the door behind them and returned to her chair, book momentarily forgotten. Her thoughts drifted to Manjit and the assessment she was about to undergo, hoping that it would bring the help and support she needed.

CHAPTER 12

~MICHELLE & MANJIT~

Manjit entered Michelle's office accompanied by Chloe. Michelle greeted them then dismissed Chloe who smiled and left the room, leaving Manjit alone with Michelle.

In the low-lit office, ambient lighting set the mood. The focal point was an oak desk, which gave off an air of elegance and sophistication. Behind the desk was a large comfortable chair specifically reserved for Michelle. The chair's size and design suggested that it was meant to provide a sense of authority and comfort for Michelle during her work. Adjacent to the large chair was a smaller quilted chair, perfect for guests or visitors. That chair offered a touch of cosiness and hospitality, inviting individuals to sit and engage in conversation.

The desk was diligently organised with various compartments and drawers neatly arranged to hold stationary, files, and other essential items. A sleek computer monitor sat at the centre of the desk, accompanied by a keyboard and mouse. A few tastefully chosen personal items, such as a family photo and a small potted plant, added a touch of warmth to the otherwise professional space. The walls were full of framed degrees, certifications, and professional achievements, showcasing her expertise and accomplishments. A few pieces of artwork and motivational quotes were strategically placed to inspire and uplift Michelle during her workday.

Bookshelves lined one wall, filled with a curated collection of books related to Michelle's field of expertise. The books served as both a resource for her and a testament to her knowledge and passion for her work in philosophy. The shelves also displayed a few decorative items including a ceramic figure of a brain. Large windows which allowed natural light to filter into the office and offer a view of the surrounding environment. However, the windows were covered with closed blinds. A comfortable seating area near the windows provided a cosy spot for Michelle to take a break, read a book, or simply enjoy the view.

To enhance the overall ambiance, the office featured a soft, muted colour palette, with neutral tones and subtle accents. The floor was carpeted with a stylish area rug that added comfort and reduced noise.

Meanwhile, Michelle took a moment to pour herself a cup of coffee. "Would you like a drink, Manjit?"

"Yes, please. A strong coffee with no sugar, thanks."

Michelle gestured for Manjit to take a seat while she prepared the coffee. As Manjit waited, her attention was drawn to a large poster on a wooden stand next to Michelle's desk. Curious, she walked closer and began to read it out loud, "What is the biblical definition of suffering? Suffering is a product of the fall, a consequence of human sin against God." Manjit continued, absorbing the words, "Suffering is in our lives because we are living in a broken world. Some suffering is due to our sinful and wrong choices, but some is due simply to the world being fallen."

Michelle expressed her opinion by saying, "No one deserves to suffer."

Manjit deduced, "It's missed out, illnesses. My world is far from broken, and I've always tried to make the right choices; the wrong ones, I've learned from. So I don't agree with that."

Michelle placed two cups of coffee on the desk and whispered, "There you go." Manjit thanked her, and Michelle opened some files on her desk. Michelle contemplated the poster's message and remarked, "Maybe the choices it's referring to, is that people don't always pay attention to their health until it's too late." Then she leaned back into her grandiose chair. Michelle playfully swung her grand office chair around then swished it back to face her desk. She continued, "I'm not at all insinuating you made the wrong choice. Terminal breast cancer?"

Manjit scowled at Michelle, feeling offended by the question. Michelle quickly realised Manjit was easily offended and the tension in the room grew insolent. The air blew fiercely with silence as both women exchanged heated glances.

Manjit flashed back to when she discovered her death was imminent...

The Blossom Breast Clinic was a serene and welcoming medical facility specifically designed to cater to the unique needs of patients seeking breast health services. Situated in the heart of a small city, its exterior featured a contemporary architectural design.

A spacious and elegantly decorated area greeted patients upon arrival. The centrally located admissions desk was staffed by friendly and smartly dressed receptionists, ensuring easy access for patients seeking assistance or check-in. The reception area was designed to provide privacy and comfort while maintaining an open and airy environment. Soft classical music played in the background, contributing to a peaceful setting.

As Manjit approached, the receptionist asked, "Can I help?"

Manjit responded, "Hi, I've got an appointment at 12:30 p.m. My name is Manjit Pojab." The receptionist checked her computer and confirmed, "That's with Dr Harris. Just wait over there. Take a seat, and someone will be with you shortly."

Manjit thanked her and looked for a seat.

Opposite the reception area was the spacious and well-appointed waiting area boasting a harmonious blend of comfort and privacy. The layout was designed to offer a sense of relaxation and reassurance to patients and their loved ones. Large windows allowed light to filter in and offered a delightful view of the small green yard.

The waiting area was furnished with a variety of seating options that included comfortable armchairs and cosy sofas arranged to provide ample personal space. Soft, plain tones that created a calming effect were used throughout the decor. soothing music drifted from discreetly placed speakers

The waiting area was also equipped with magazines, brochures, and educational materials related to breast health, empowering patients with information and promoting awareness. A small refreshment station offered a selection of complimentary beverages and light snacks, ensuring patients felt cared for during their wait. To respect patient privacy, the waiting area incorporated designated consultation rooms where doctors could meet with patients individually for preliminary discussions or to provide test results. These private spaces were soundproofed and furnished with comfortable seating, ensuring confidentiality and fostering open communication.

As Manjit relaxed in her seat, her mobile phone rang. She checked the screen and saw Sarah on the other end. Manjit excitedly took her call, and they engaged in conversation as Sarah suggested meeting for coffee at lunch. Manjit regretted that she couldn't make it that day, but proposed to meet tomorrow instead.

Sarah confirmed their plans and then asked about their scheduled outing on Saturday, mentioning that she had already booked a table. Manjit assured her that she would be there and promised to call her later. They said their goodbyes and hung up.

She opened a shopping app on her phone and continued adding items to her basket, such as milk and other essentials. A nurse entered the waiting area and called out, "Manjit Pojab?"

Manjit quietly yelped, "Yes, that's me."

The nurse instructed her to follow and led her into a room where she asked Manjit to take a seat then proceeded to check her computer and the notes in her folder.

The nurse confirmed the reason for Manjit's referral, enquiring, "So your doctor has referred you for a lump on your left breast?"

Manjit acknowledged this, explaining, "Yes, that's right, just for precaution really."

The nurse then politely asked Manjit to remove her

top and bra, ensuring privacy by closing the curtain. Manjit was instructed to sit on the bed when she was ready. Manjit complied, and the nurse continued with her examination. Afterwards, Manjit found herself in the stark and sterile environment of the mammogram room. As she sat there, her face portrayed no emotion. The room was filled with a large mammogram machine, it created an eerie symphony of soft clanks and twirls. It seemed as though the very walls were vibrating with the rhythmic hum of the apparatus. Manjit's heart raced in sync with the discrete beats, her anxiety growing with each passing second.

The radiologist, clad in a white lab coat, moved around the room with practised efficiency. Gloved hands adjusted the machine, positioning Manjit's breast carefully between the two plates. The ordeal was uncomfortable, the pressure exerted on her chest caused a dull ache. But she remained still, determined to endure whatever was necessary for her health. As the machine whirred into action, the room was active with a series of clicks and electronic beeps. X-rays of Manjit's breast appeared on the computer screen as a black and white image that revealed the inner workings of her tissues.

Lines and shadows danced across the screen, forming a map of her breast that only a trained eye could decipher.

Manjit's gaze never wavered from the screen, her focus intensely even as the machine continued its mechanical symphony. She watched as the technician reviewed the images, eyes scanning intently for any abnormalities or signs of concern. Time seemed to stand still as the seconds ticked by, every passing moment stretching into eternity. Finally, the radiologist turned to Manjit with a reassuring smile.

"All done," she said, her voice breaking through the tension in the room. Manjit felt relief, her shoulders relaxed as the worry lifted from them. She nodded and hope shined in her eyes as she thanked the radiologist. Slowly, she climbed down from the examination table to dress, the coldness of the room faded as she stepped back into the corridor. The starkness of the mammogram room remained clear in her mind, a reminder of her resilience and the importance of regular check-ups.

Manjit sat and waited anxiously before the doctor called her. Manjit entered the doctor's room where he had reviewed the notes containing the results of her diagnostic mammogram and ultrasound. His face wore a grave expression as he absorbed the information. Breaking the heavy silence, Dr Harris began to speak, "I'm really sorry to inform you, Ms. Pojab, the tests have detected an infiltrating lobular carcinoma."

Manjit's eyes sank with fright. "It's not cancer, is it?" she uttered, desperately hoping for a different answer.

Dr Harris's expression saddened, "I'm afraid it is. The tests have confirmed the presence of cancer. Unfortunately, the tumour has spread..." Manjit's heart skipped a beat, and she froze in silence. The extent of those words felt as if her presence was nothing more than an illusion. Manjit struggled to process the devastating news. Her mind raced with questions and disbelief, a sense of uncertainty clouding her thoughts.

Manjit's world shattered as she desperately sought answers from Dr Harris. Her voice quivered as she asked the question that plunged deep in her heart.

"What stage is it?" her voice barely above a whisper.

Dr Harri's sombre expression revealed the harsh reality she was facing. "Stage 4, advanced," he responded with genuine regret.

Those words hit Manjit like a freight train. The extent and reality of the situation slowly sank in, and she couldn't help but voice her deepest fear, "So, I'm going to die?" She trembled with resignation, hoping this was just a dreadful mistake. Dr Harris' gaze softened, understanding the immense anguish she was experiencing. "It's terminal," he confirmed gently.

The air deepened with an unbearable silence as Manjit grappled with the devastating truth. Her mind raced, trying to comprehend the limited time she had left. "How long?" Dr Harris took a breath. His delay in answering created dark lingering thoughts.

"Due to how invasive and fast-growing the tumour is, you're looking at months, a year tops," he explained, "I know it's an awful shock for you." His words that moment had been repeated so many times, and with each patient he witnessed the same unforgettable reaction of horror, which made his job emotionally challenging.

Manjit sat frozen, her body petrified by the reality that was unfolding before her. Tears welled up in her eyes as she struggled to process the magnitude of the situation.

Dr Harris, understanding the overwhelming emotions Manjit was experiencing, continued speaking softly, "I'm happy to answer any questions you may have?" he offered. "Do you have anyone you can call? I can talk you through the palliative care process if you think you're ready."

Still reeling from the devastating news she received at the hospital, Manjit tried to find solace in the familiarity of her home. She stood alone in her kitchen, a reflection of her refined taste and love for all things culinary. It was her special place.

The countertops, also made of granite, lined the perimeter of the kitchen, providing ample space for food preparation. Manjit took great pride in her collection of high-quality knives, neatly arranged on a magnetic strip attached to the tiled backsplash. A row of gleaming stainless-steel appliances, including a state-of-the-art stove, refrigerator, and dishwasher, further enhanced the kitchen's modern aesthetic.

A large, farmhouse-style sink sat beneath a window, offering a picturesque view of the garden outside. Manjit often found comfort in this view, watching the colourful blooms sway gently in the breeze as she tackled culinary challenges. The kitchen was filled with subtle touches of personalisation. A collection of aromatic herbs had grown in small pots on a windowsill, ready to be plucked and added to Manjit's creations. Vibrant artwork depicting food and nature covered the walls, adding a splash of colour to the otherwise neutral palette.

As Manjit mechanically prepared her coffee, her glare often drifted to the stainless-steel refrigerator with subtly placed magnets and photos, reminding her of cherished memories. The coffee machine hissed, and the smell of freshly brewed coffee flowed in the air. But that day, they failed to provide the comfort she desperately craved. Despite the elegance and functionality of Manjit's kitchen, it felt empty and cold without the joy and laughter that once blossomed in the space.

The devastating news she received at the hospital weighed heavily on her heart, casting a shadow over the room that was once the heart of her home. As she carried the steaming cup, Manjit walked through the hallway filled with family photos and certificates proudly displayed on the walls. The photos captured precious moments with loved ones, preserving memories of happier times. Among them, Manjit's achievements were showcased, two degrees in Business & Finance and Law, both bearing her name.

She entered the lounge, where a deluxe

contemporary sofa awaited her. The room exuded warmth and familiarity, but on that day, it felt like nothing but an empty tomb. Manjit sank into the soft cushions, her thoughts consumed by her diagnosis.

A bookshelf stood against one wall, filled with a diverse assortment of books. From classic literature to contemporary novels, a set of business books, self-help guides to philosophical treatises, the collection was a testament to Manjit's thirst for knowledge and intellectual curiosity. The shelves also housed mementos from her travels, delicate porcelain figurines, and small trinkets that held sentimental value.

A large, ornate coffee table sat in the centre of the room, covered with carefully arranged books and magazines. The table's surface was a kaleidoscope of colours, as it showcased a vibrant bouquet of fresh flowers, which were carefully arranged in an elegant vase. The sweet scent of the blossoms consumed the air, adding a touch of nature's beauty to the space. Near the window, a set of plush armchairs and a small side table created a cosy reading nook. A soft woven blanket was neatly draped over one of the chairs, inviting Manjit to wrap herself in its warmth and find relief within the pages of a favourite book. Sunlight filtered through the curtains of this lavish space.

As Manjit took another sip of her steaming cup, she couldn't help but feel the contrast between the physical comfort of her surroundings and the emotional turmoil within. The room, once a sanctuary of peace and contentment, now felt like a dying existence, mirroring the emptiness she was feeling in her heart. Her thoughts wandered back to the family photos on the hallway walls, reminding her of the love and support that had always surrounded her. The certificates represented the hard-earned accomplishments which had offered some meaning to her life; they were a reminder of her strength and dreams. At that moment, Manjit found herself caught between the past and an uncertain future. She clung to the familiar sights and sounds of her lounge, searching for hope and inspiration to face the challenges ahead.

Just as she began to lose herself in the solitude of her thoughts, her landline phone interrupted the silence, jarring her back to the present moment. With curiosity and dread, she picked up the phone, and her heartbeat quickened. Manjit's hand wobbled slightly as she brought the phone to her ear, uncertain of who might be calling and what news they might bring. It was Manjit's mother, Sudi, asking if everything was all right. Manjit assured her that she had been busy with work and apologised for not calling her. Sudi asked Manjit about the hospital visit. Manjit replied, "Fine, Mum." However, her tone indicated that something was obviously troubling her.

She asked if everything was clear, causing Manjit to hesitate and hold back tears. Sudi persisted and asked what was wrong. Manjit, trying to compose herself, replied that it was okay and abruptly ended the conversation, telling her mum she had to go. After hanging up, Manjit took a sip of her coffee. Her hands started shaking, and she couldn't hold back her tears any longer. Hastily, she placed the coffee cup back down.

Feeling overwhelmed, Manjit walked towards a large mirror that hung on her wall. She gawked solemnly at her reflection, trying hard to control her emotions. However, the effort became too much, and she let out a scream, releasing the pent-up anguish she had been holding inside.

Manjit's mother called again. Between sobs, Manjit responded, "I'll tell you later, Mum." Deep down, she knew she couldn't keep it to herself any longer. She took a deep breath and steadied herself, wiping away her tears and preparing to face the difficult conversation she'd sooner avoid. Battling with her new dark reality, she knew it was time to confide in her mother and share the burden she was carrying.

CHAPTER 13

~LAUGHTER AND ANGER~

Meanwhile, the evening grew darker. Dave and Claire sat together in her room, enjoying their time before their last night on Earth. Dave suggested they made the most of it, and they shared laughter as they tapped their cups together. Claire raised her cup and proposed a toast, "Here's to our last night on planet Earth." They both downed their drinks, savouring the moment.

Dave then suggested going exploring, perhaps to make the most of their remaining time. Claire responded with a touch of sarcasm, remarking, "Exploring? We're not on a bloody safari!"

Dave, undeterred, suggested they should look around the building, half-jokingly hoping to find some dead bodies.

Claire laughed at his dark humour, "You're funny.

Sick, but funny."

Dave's tone turned serious as he wondered out loud where all the dead bodies might be. Claire, still in a light-hearted mood, playfully replied, "Who? Dead bodies? They might be in the garden having a fag."

Dave added to the joking atmosphere by suggesting they could ask the imaginary dead bodies for a cigarette. They both erupted in laughter, sharing a moment of dark humour in the face of their uncertain circumstances.

As the evening unfolded, Manjit returned to her room where she could hear laughter emanating from Claire's room nearby. Angrily, she looked at Sudi and remarked about the sound of laughter coming from Claire's room. Sudi speculated that perhaps Claire found the idea of dying funny, which prompted disapproval from Manjit, who found it disrespectful. Shifting the topic, Sudi asked Manjit about her appointment. Manjit responded casually, mentioning that she had just had a surreal chat and then signed her life away, dismissing the lack of seriousness in the situation. Not amused by the remark, Sudi offered Manjit a coffee, to which Manjit agreed. Sudi proceeded to prepare the drinks while Manjit settled on the bed, patiently waiting for her coffee.

Sudi inquired if Manjit was hungry. She said no, but suggested they could grab something to eat if Sudi was hungry. Sudi declined, mentioning that she had brought her own snacks which would suffice for the night.

Sudi handed Manjit her drink, and sat on the bed, holding her own cup in her hands. The intensity of the situation hung in the air as they tried to find peace in each other's company. Manjit smiled softly at her mother's persistence and sat closer to her on the couch. The room was immersed with the comforting scent of coffee. "Thanks, Mum," Manjit said with warmth sparkling in her eyes.

Sudi whispered to her daughter, her voice filled with both anticipation and apprehension, urging Manjit to share everything. She expressed her desire to understand and emphasised her wish to know her daughter fully, without any secrets.

Manjit sighed, her fingers absentmindedly rubbing her temple as she stared into her coffee cup. Sudi continued to delve, "When I asked why you hadn't met anyone? You said..." she paused, collecting her thoughts.

"Does it really matter now, Mum? We should just enjoy this time we have together," Manjit remarked as she sipped on her coffee. Sudi insisted on knowing the truth.

Manjit, after a deep breath to compose herself, gathered the courage to reveal her truth to her mother. With a heavy heart, she confessed, "I'm gay, Mum. Sarah and I have been in a relationship for 5 years now."

Upon hearing this revelation, Sudi's face showed signs of sadness. Manjit, noticing her mother's reaction, felt regret seep into her voice as she expressed her apprehension about sharing this truth. Sudi's voice trembled as she tried to come to terms with the news, struggling to process the unexpected revelation and the new reality it presented.

Manjit's frustration mounted, prompting her to rise from her seat and begin pacing the room in agitation. She expressed her premonition that her mother would never accept her truth, recounting the burden of living a falsehood and emphasising that being gay was not a choice she made. Sudi, still struggling to comprehend, attempted to clarify by asking if Manjit did not like men.

Manjit's face displayed frustration and regret as she compared her sexual orientation to an uncontrollable affliction like cancer, reiterating that she was gay and solely attracted to women. Despite feeling disheartened by the situation, she reiterated softly that being gay was not a choice she made.

Sensing the escalating tension, Sudi called out to her daughter, prompting Manjit to pause in her movements and reluctantly return to sit beside her mother. Sudi, reaching out to hold Manjit's hand gently, gazed at her with eyes filled with love and acceptance. She reassured Manjit that her attraction did not matter, emphasising that she was her beloved daughter, and that was all that truly mattered to her.

Manjit's eyes filled with tears as she expressed her protest, her voice tinged with doubt. She believed that the words spoken were influenced by the fact that it was their final night together. Sudi's grasp on her hand tightened, providing a steady and supportive presence. Manjit, tears streaming down her face, indicated her understanding of this reality.

Sudi's voice took on a gentler tone, reflecting a profound comprehension of the situation. She observed that in the current moment, these concerns seemed less relevant, offering a new perspective on the matter at hand. Considering the impact of Manjit's illness, Sudi alluded to the potential for a different perspective or course of action.

All Sudi wished for was Manjit's happiness. Manjit posed a question, asking if Sudi would still desire her happiness even if it meant being in a gay relationship. Sudi's gaze locked with Manjit's, unwavering and filled with unconditional love. She affirmed her stance, stating that nothing could alter Manjit's essence, and she would always remember her remarkable qualities. The two embraced each other tightly, tears blending together. In that poignant moment, the barriers of misunderstanding dissolved, giving way to a connection that surpassed societal labels and preconceived notions.

CHAPTER 14

~MICHELLE AND CLAIRE~

Later that evening, Chloe stood outside Claire's door, and her knuckles rapped lightly against the wood. A moment later, the door opened, revealing Claire's flustered face. She soon realised she had her meeting with Michelle and scolded herself for forgetting about the assessment and invited Chloe in. Chloe noticed Dave and the vodka.

"Dave, you're next," Chloe announced, her eyes twinkling with suspicion. "Where will you be in around half an hour?"

Dave rose from his seat, momentarily disoriented by the sudden attention. He stumbled over Claire's bag, which had been carelessly left in his path. He regained his balance, his face flushed.

"Er...," Dave stammered and tried to compose himself. His gaze shifted to Claire.

Chloe, ever observant, caught the connection between Dave and Claire. A cheeky smile played on her lips as she decided to seize the moment.

"Stay here," Claire insisted, with a hint of mischief, "I'm not going to be long." She made her way to the door with Chloe following closely behind. Chloe sensed Claire's nervousness, so she placed a comforting hand on her shoulder.

"Don't worry, Claire. Michelle is there to help us, not to judge us."

Claire managed a small smile, grateful for Chloe's support. She knew Chloe was right. The assessment was an opportunity for them to discuss the procedure.

Before their arrival, Michelle sat at her desk sipping gin. She began tapping her fingers impatiently on the smooth surface. With a quick command, she summoned the power of technology. "Alexa, play...music."

Alexa, the voice command, reacted with a robotic voice, "Playing the top 50 music hits."

A song, 'Flowers' by Macey Lee, played. Unable to resist the urge to dance, Michelle jumped out of her chair where she lost herself in the rhythm of the music. She twirled and swayed, her movements synchronised with the melody. In the midst of her joyful dance, she took a large sip from her silver tanker, relishing the refreshing taste. Suddenly she heard muffled voices coming from somewhere nearby. Her senses heightened, without wasting another moment, she swiftly requested, "Alexa, stop."

The music immediately halted. Michelle sprang into action, her eyes darted around the room until they landed on her desk drawer. Michelle's heart raced as she hurriedly opened her desk drawer and carefully placed her secret silver tanker inside. It was the escape she treasured dearly. Just as she closed the drawer, there was a knock at her office door, which caused her to startle. Taking a deep breath, Michelle quickly straightened her clothes, smoothing out any wrinkles and ensuring she looked presentable. She ran her fingers through her hair, attempting to tame any stray strands that might have escaped during her skilful moves. With a composed demeanour, she walked briskly towards the door and opened it, revealing her employee standing on the other side.

"Hi there," she greeted, her tone carrying an air of professionalism, "Please come in, Claire."

Claire entered the room.

"Claire! Lovely to meet you again," she exclaimed. Her cheery nature slightly overwhelmed Claire.

Claire responded with a simple "Hi" then took a seat when Michelle invited her to do so. While Claire settled in, her eyes wandered to a poster displayed on a stand nearby.

Michelle noticed Claire's interest and spoke up, breaking the silence, "The biblical definition of suffering." she announced, acknowledging that it was a poster that often caught people's attention. Claire continued to read the poster intently, absorbing its contents.

Michelle, eager to engage in conversation, offered Claire a drink. Claire politely declined so Michelle took her seat, ready to delve into a deeper discussion.

"No one needs to suffer, do they?" she pondered with conviction, but Claire was still fixated on the poster.

She finally responded defensively, "I didn't choose to have depression." Her words carried a hint of vulnerability, expressing the complexity of her emotions. Michelle considered Claire's response.

"No, but what if the events in your past led to a series of downpours, ultimately causing depression?" she suggested, exploring the possibility of external factors contributing to Claire's condition.

Claire took her eyes away from the poster, turned her attention to Michelle, and offered her an alternative perspective. "What if it's an unbalanced chemical in the brain? Which could be genetic?" she challenged, highlighting the potential biological roots of depression. Michelle was taken aback by Claire's response. She hesitated for a moment before speaking again. "Erm, is that what you really think?" uninterested in Claire's viewpoint.

Claire's gaze returned to the poster, with a bemused expression. "Does it really matter?" she implied that the cause of depression may be less significant than finding ways to cope and heal.

Michelle nodded, accepting Claire's perspective. "No, but I'm always interested in what causes people to feel depressed," she continued, "I believe the main cause is unresolved childhood trauma."

The conversation hung awkwardly in the air.

She looked at Michelle, brows caved inwards with annoyance and she sought clarification, "Okay, but what's this got to do with anything?"

Michelle, with a gentle yet determined tone, responded, "You can talk to me. I can see your trauma." Her words of understanding and empathy felt artificial.

"What?" she demanded, her voice raised with frustration.

Michelle leaned forward, her expression falsely portraying kindness and compassion. "What happened?" she wondered. Michelle invited Claire to open up to her, "Talk to me Claire, please? Start from the beginning. Let's be open."

Claire hesitated, confused by Michelle's character. Her mind flooded with a myriad of emotions and memories. She looked into Michelle's eyes, where she searched and hoped for a genuine willingness to listen and support her. With a deep breath, Claire reluctantly began to share her story, starting from the earliest recollection of her past. As the words spilled out, Claire felt a weight had been lifted from her shoulders.

Michelle, fascinated and curious about other people's pain and suffering, intently listened. She tried to offer words of encouragement and understanding along the way.

The barriers that had once held Claire back began to

crumble, which allowed her to scrabble into the depths of her experiences and confront the pain that had long haunted her. In that moment, Claire naively felt a connection rooted in vulnerability and shared humanity. Her defensiveness disappeared, and feeling content and safe, the room unexpectedly transformed into a sanctuary where Claire could unburden herself and Michelle could offer solace and guidance. In the safety of that intimate space, without noticing Michelle's deadpan stares, she flashed back to some of the main events from her past...

Thirteen-year-old Claire, dressed in her school uniform, walked out of the school gates, her shoulders slumped and her gaze fixed on the ground. As she made her way home, a group of schoolgirls noticed her and cruelly taunted her, their laughter piercing through the air. "Look at her socks and skirt," Girl A sneered, unable to contain her amusement.

"She doesn't have any friends," added Girl B, her words dripping with disdain. "I'm not surprised. Fat cow," chimed in Girl C, her words laced with malice.

Girl D, the most aggressive of the group, called out to Claire, her voice filled with mockery, "Oi, Fatty! Do you wanna smoke with us? Don't ignore me."

Feeling overwhelmed and scared, Claire quickened her pace, desperate to escape the torment. She ran home, her heart pounding, seeking safety. She finally arrived, panting and on the verge of tears. As the girls continued their walk, their mocking words echoing in the distance, Claire reached her front door. She gasped as she tried to catch a breath to steady herself before mustering the courage to turn the doorknob. With a thundering heart and tears streaming down her face, she stepped into the familiar embrace of the lounge.

Inside, the room with familiar furniture covered her in a semblance of comfort. Yet even within the sanctuary of her home, the wounds inflicted by the hurtful words and laughter lingered, etching themselves deep within her fragile spirit.

Claire abruptly closed the door. Her mother slouched on the sofa engrossed in her favourite television program. Oblivious to Claire's presence she didn't acknowledge her daughter's attempt to get her attention.

"Mum?" Claire called out, hoping for a response.

Without tearing her eyes away from the TV, her mother replied in a hushed tone, "SSh! If you want anything to eat, there's toast or cereal."

Frustration washed over her, and Claire expressed her discontent, "I hate school, Mum! I hate people!"

Her mother, still fixated on the television, abruptly interrupted, "Shut up."

Claire persisted, hoping for some understanding, "But Mum! I hate it when everyone is mean to me."

Growing impatient, her mother finally turned her towards Claire, her annoyance evident in her voice, "Leave me alone! You're always bloody moaning. Everything upsets you. It's pathetic."

Heartbroken by her mother's lack of empathy, Claire retreated to her room feeling unheard and misunderstood, which was often.

Claire's memories are disturbed when Michelle intervenes. "Ah, see, I knew it. Childhood issues." Michelle's words left Claire perplexed and upset.

"I haven't said anything wrong, have I?" Michelle queried, noticing Claire's disapproval.

Claire shook her head and replied, "No, I'm just confused, why would you say that?" Michelle, realising her insensitivity and questioning was something she needed to conceal better, reached a comforting hand out to Claire, "I'm sorry, Claire. I didn't mean to belittle or oversimplify your experiences. I should have been more considerate and understanding. I stupidly say the wrong things sometimes. Please, don't stop sharing."

Claire deliberated mindfully, contemplating Michelle's sincerity. With a build up of willpower to offload her recent troubles with her mum, she hesitated no further and went to a recent memory...

In a small grimy flat, which appeared to be consumed and dampened with neglect, the room was dimly lit with only a feeble ray of sunlight filtering through a thin, tattered curtain. The once-painted white walls were stained and marked by the passage of time. The floor was strewn with clothes, tangled in a chaotic mess as if they were hastily discarded in a moment of apathy. Dirty plates and half-eaten meals occupied the limited countertop space which was caked with dried remains of forgotten meals. The sight and smell of decaying food lingered in the air, a reminder of the neglect that had shadowed this space. Empty cups, some with residue of stale liquids, were scattered haphazardly on the kitchen table, the surface marked with rings of abandonment.

The furniture in the room was worn and dilapidated, its upholstery faded and torn. A threadbare couch sat against one wall, sagging under the weight of age and neglect. The coffee table in front of it was covered in a layer of dust with empty food containers and crumpled papers scattered on its surface. A rickety wooden bookshelf stood in one corner, its shelves cluttered with books and magazines that hadn't been touched in years. The pages had yellowed with time and some curled at the edges. The titles ranged from discovery to fictional books. A small, makeshift kitchenette occupied another corner of the room. The countertop there was also cluttered with unwashed dishes and empty food containers. The sink was stained and clogged with grime, emitting a faint odour of decay. A small stove sat adjacent to the sink, its burners covered in grease and grime.

The room was completely devoid of personal touches or decorations, except for a few faded photographs hanging crookedly on the walls. The faces captured in the pictures were blurry and indistinct, their identities lost to the passage of time. Overall, the atmosphere in the room felt like a forgotten space. It was a place that had been abandoned, physically and emotionally, leaving behind a palpable sense of loneliness and decay.

The lack of cleanliness and order reflected a deep sense of indifference and a loss of motivation. A home which seemed devoid of life, as if it had succumbed to its own desolation. It was a stark reminder of the toll that carelessness and disarray can take on one's physical and mental well-being. The room yearned and screamed for a breath of fresh air, a cleansing light to chase away the shadows and breathe life back into its forgotten corners.

Suddenly there was a knock at the door, interrupting Claire's peaceful afternoon. Reluctantly, she got up from the couch and made her way to the front door. Opening it, she was greeted by her mother's familiar face.

"Mum?" Claire said, surprised.

"Well, aren't you clever," her mother replied, stepping into the flat. She looked around, her eyes full of disgust, "Bloody hell, Claire, don't you ever clean up? This is just dirty."

Claire's mother inspected the mess, making her way into the small kitchen that faced the lounge. Meanwhile, Claire slumped back down on the couch and resumed watching TV. "Fuck me, I can't get my head around this," her mother remarked, picking up unopened letters from the table, "These are bills! You haven't even opened them?" Her voice grew louder as she called out, "Hello, are you in there somewhere?"

"Just leave it. It's fine," Claire responded dismissively.

Her mother couldn't believe what she was hearing. "Fine," she says, ignoring Claire's request.

Claire yelled back to her mum, "I said leave it." After an uncomfortable pause, Claire asked, "What do you want anyway? Apart from inspecting my flat." Her mother sighed, "Well, that's nice. I didn't expect to pay you a visit and walk into a bloody shit hole again. Something's wrong with you. You're like a zombie."

"I never asked you to visit," Claire retorted.

"Well, since you can't be arsed to visit me, I thought it'd be nice to surprise you," her mother yelled with sarcasm.

"Surprise me," Claire muttered under her breath.

Her mother ignored her sarcastic tone, "I don't know why I even bother. I'm dying for a cuppa, but I suppose I'll have to wait until I get home. Not that I'd want one in this filth hole."

Growing tired of the conversation, Claire simply

agreed, "Bye, then."

"Sort yourself out," her mother said angrily, "You sit around all day doing sod all. You don't ever want to do anything."

"How many times do I need to hear it?" Claire snapped.

Her mother paused for a moment, then sighed, "Well, it's a waste of breath." And with that, she turned and left, leaving Claire alone in her messy flat. Feeling huge amounts of frustration and sadness after her mother's visit, Claire got up from the couch and made her way towards the window. She needed a moment of comfort, a chance to collect her thoughts and escape the tension that lingered in the air.

Standing by the window, she solemnly stared outside, her gaze fixed on the world beyond her flat. The streets looked happy with life, oblivious to the turmoil within her. People hurriedly went about their business, cars zoomed by, and the distant sounds of the town distracted her thoughts. Claire found life in the outside world a temporary escape from the anguish of her problems. As she stared into the distance, her mind wandered, contemplating the state of her life. The messiness of her flat was a mere reflection of the chaos within. She knew her mother's words held some truth, even if they were delivered with harshness. It wasn't just about the bills and the unopened letters; it was about the bigger picture, the stagnation that seemed to consume her.

Claire's thoughts drifted to the dreams she once had, the aspirations that had seemed to slip away with each passing day. She yearned for a sense of purpose, a renewed motivation to make something of herself. But it was easier said than done when she felt trapped in a cycle of emotional and mental pain. The outside world continued its relentless pace, unaffected by Claire's internal struggle. The sight of people going about their lives, pursuing their dreams, served as a bittersweet reminder of what she felt she was missing. She longed for a spark, a catalyst to break free from the monotony that had enveloped her existence. Claire took in the scene with deep sadness, observing the interactions between an old man, a mother, and a young child, the warm exchange between them filled with positivity and joy.

The sun's rays illuminated the day, creating a vibrant atmosphere that seemed to enhance the happiness of the people around. As Claire continued to watch, she noticed other individuals and groups enjoying the day. Friends laughing together on a park bench, couples strolling hand in hand, and families playing games on the grass. The sound of children's laughter flowed through the air, blending with the cheerful conversations of passersby made Claire feel more lonely.

With a sigh, Claire turned away from the window. Her eyes shifted back to her cluttered flat. The messiness seemed to mirror the clutter in her mind, a physical manifestation of her emotional state. Deep down, she knew that something needed to change. It was time to confront her own demons, to find the strength to clean up not just her physical space, but also the disarray within herself.

Taking a deep breath, Claire vowed to take the first step towards resolving her pain. It wouldn't be easy and the road ahead was uncertain, but she couldn't continue living in this stagnant state. With newfound determination, she turned away from the window and set her sights on the task forward. Claire picked up her phone and began to dial a number.

She waited anxiously as the phone continued to ring.

Her heart pounded in her chest, and she nervously bit her nails, a clear sign of her unease. The seconds felt like an eternity as she waited for someone to pick up. Finally, a voice answered, and Claire's breath caught in her throat. She inhaled then exhaled, taking a long breath, trying to steady herself. She knew this conversation was important, and her choice to dial number 2 on her phone indicated that she had a specific person in mind.

As she listened to the voice on the line, her expression shifted, revealing a glimmer of hope and trepidation. The conversation unfolded, and Claire's emotions became more apparent with every second of every minute. Her detached, dejected face started to show signs of vulnerability as she engaged into a conversation.

The world beyond her window faded away as Claire became fully engrossed in the exchange. She spoke with words of hesitation, conveying her thoughts and feelings in a way only she could understand. Claire's phone remained firmly clutched in her hand as she continued to navigate the discussion. The window beside her, which was fogged up from her heavy breathing, served as a canvas for her emotions. She absentmindedly traced her finger over the steamed fog and drew a sad face, a reflection of her current state of mind.

Claire rapidly sat up and anxiously awaited a response, troubled by Michelle's clock-watching. Looking to improvise her next words, Michelle distracted Claire by telling her, "Sadly the world is a broken place."

Claire expressed her belief that it was the people who were broken, not the world itself. Michelle argued that it was the people who were responsible for the state of the world.

"Humanity is a disappointment," Claire sighed, her voice deepened with resentment. Michelle nodded in agreement, "I agree, but only with the ones we've already met," she declared, her tone tinged with cynicism.

Claire maintained her stance, "All the same, greedy and dishonest."

Michelle was thrown by Claire's sudden empowerment. She paused before answering, contemplating Claire's question, "Every one of us has a nasty side. Do you?"

Claire wasted no time in firing her answer, "I feel angry. Let down. And I think in a situation where I was pushed, I could be nasty."

Their eyes met, and Claire could sense a flicker of intimidation in Michelle's glare. "All my life, I've allowed others to push me around, belittle and humiliate me," Claire confessed, her voice filled with vulnerability and determination, "There's only so much a person can take." Michelle's boredom was out of sight as she scowled at her drawer, desperate for a sneaky sip of gin. Suddenly, she swung around in her chair, facing Claire directly, "Fighting talk, I like it!" She shouted, a hint of mockery in her voice. She banged her fist loudly on her desk, emphasising her words, "Now that's what I'm talking about."

Claire was taken aback by Michelle's sudden change in demeanour. She couldn't help but feel bewildered by the situation. "So, is this my assessment?" she asked, seeking clarity. Michelle nodded, an impish glint in her eyes. "Part of it, yes," she confirmed, "I have some forms for you to sign, Claire." Rummaging through a pile of papers, Michelle finally found the documents she was looking for. "Ah, here we are," she called out, "Sign here if you're happy to go ahead with tomorrow and then here, for kindly donating your organs."

Claire was sceptical for a moment while her mind

raced with mistrustfulness. However, after experiencing Michelle's bizarre and altered personality, her eagerness to leave the office quickly swayed her decision. Without further ado, she picked up the pen. Michelle couldn't contain her excitement. "Just sign here, dear," she insisted, with a playful smirk on her face. "Ha! That rhymed."

Claire signed the forms, unaware of the potential consequences. Claire couldn't help wondering if she had made a terrible mistake. But the decision had been made.

Claire returned to her room, her footsteps drumming loudly onto the floor, indicating her troubles. Dave, who had been nervously waiting, sipped the remnants of his vodka. He quickly set the glass down, trying to position himself.

"It's your turn," Claire stated matter-of-factly, her voice carrying a hint of amusement.

Dave looked up at her, his eyes glazed with uncertainty. "Was it okay?" he asked with hope and anxiety.

Claire nodded, a slight grin jiggled on her lips. "I don't know," she confided, confused. "She's bloody wacky, but it's fine, I guess. Chloe is waiting outside."

Dave let out a sigh of relief, and a smile broke across his face, "Great, see you in a bit then?"

Claire nodded again, hoping her mixed expression gave Dave some reassurance. "Yeah, I'll wait here for you," she cheerily projected. With that, Dave walked out of the room, his spirits lifted. He felt a renewed sense of confidence, knowing that Claire had approved the interaction with the enigmatic woman she had recently encountered. As he made his way towards Chloe, who patiently waited outside, he couldn't help but feel a sense of anticipation for what lay ahead. Little did he know that this night would mark the beginning of an unforgettable journey, one that would test his limits and change his life in ways he could never have imagined.

CHAPTER 15

~MICHELLE AND DAVE~

Michelle stood in her office, her phone propped up on the cabinet. She was engrossed in a music and dance TikTok video, captivated by the catchy rhythm and the silly moves. Unable to resist, she decided to give it a try herself. After a few quick sips of gin, Michelle placed her flask tanker under some folders. With an insidious grin on her face, Michelle attempted to replicate the dance moves, her body swaying and her limbs flailing exaggeratedly. As she got into the groove, she lost her balance for a moment, nearly stumbling and falling over. She let out a surprised giggle, grateful that no one was there to witness her near mishap.

However, just as she caught her breath and regained her composure, a knock at the door startled her. Panic washed over her face, and she quickly switched off her phone, as if the mere presence of the video would betray her moment of light-heartedness. Standing up straight, Michelle tried to regain herself, assuming a professional and serious attitude. She attempted to hide any trace of her playful antics just moments ago. She wanted to present herself as a competent and responsible individual, rather than a mischievous schoolgirl caught in the act.

As the door opened, Michelle greeted the visitor with a composed smile, ready to attend to any matters that might have arisen. Deep down, though, she couldn't help but feel a lingering sense of amusement from her secret dance session, knowing that her playful side was always ready to surface when the opportunity presented itself. Michelle stood by the open door, her voice inviting, "Well... come in," she asserted, gesturing for Chloe to enter. The door swung fully open, and Chloe greeted Michelle with a reserved smile as she stepped into the room. Following closely behind Chloe was Dave, his expression displaying both uncertainty and curiosity.

"Hello, Dave! How are you?" Michelle asked in a jolly and welcoming tone.

Dave hesitated, unsure of how to respond,

"Erm...okay?"

"Thanks my dear," Michelle smirked, as she waved goodbye to Chloe. Michelle chuckled, dismissing Dave's response with a flap of her hand. "Was that a silly question?" she queried rhetorically, her tone light-hearted. "Oh, never mind me. Take a seat. Coffee? Tea?"

Dave took a moment as he tried to gauge Michelle's playful demeanour, then decided to go with tea. "Erm...tea, please," he requested, his voice slightly indecisive. "Three sugars."

Michelle raised an eyebrow, feigning surprise. "Three sugars? What a beast!" she yelled, with a naughty spark in her eyes.

Dave was again taken aback by her comment, unsure of how to interpret it, but he didn't dare challenge her. He simply smiled politely, not wanting to disrupt the friendly, strange atmosphere.

As Michelle prepared the tea, Dave settled into a nearby chair, and his eyes wandered around the room. He couldn't shake the feeling that this encounter would be far from ordinary, so he braced himself for whatever unexpected twists and turns laid ahead.

Finally, with the drinks prepared, Michelle broke the

silence. "So, Mr. Wilson" she began, her tone shifting to a more serious and probing note, "depression, isn't it?"

Dave nodded, his eyes fixed on the cup of tea in front of him. "Yeah," he stated, his voice quietly acknowledging the truth.

Michelle continued with her line of questioning, words probing deeper into Dave's personal experiences. "Have you always had it? Depression?" Her voice was gentle yet persistent. "Would you say it's a genetic condition? Do you think life has been okay?"

Dave sat in silence for a moment, his mind grappling with the catalogue of Michelle's questions. He reflected on his experience with depression, the ups and downs, and the impact it had on his life. It was a complex and deeply personal topic, one that required careful consideration before responding.

Finally, he looked up, meeting Michelle's stare with vulnerability and introspection. "I...I think it's something I've struggled with for a long time," his voice dampened with a touch of sadness. "As for whether it's genetic or not, I'm not entirely sure. It's hard to say. And as for life...well, it's been a long slide down, to say the least." The room swept silent once again. Dave knew he was about to face some uncomfortable truths. And with Michelle's unwavering glare and curiosity, he felt a flicker of hope that perhaps the encounter would offer him a new perspective on why he was there.

Michelle proceeded to probe Dave with intrusive and sensitive queries, prodding Dave to open his silent wounds.

Not wanting to disappoint her, Dave started to unravel his past by throwing them back to a pivotal life event in his childhood …

A man and a woman stood outside an office door accompanied by a young boy named David, who was nine years old. The woman gently held David's hand as they approached the door. She looked down at David. "Please sit on one of these seats here," she instructed, pointing at the available chairs. "Stay there while we speak to Mrs. Longane. We won't be long, okay?" the woman softly said, offering David reassurance. David obediently took a seat with his head hung down. He sat in the waiting area, hands clasped tightly together, and both eyes momentarily glued on the closed door. The waiting area was a quiet and serene space, with comfortable chairs lined up against the walls.

David's eyes darted towards the door every time he heard a faint sound coming from inside the room. He listened carefully, hoping to catch any sign or indication that would suggest the imminent end of his wait. The anticipation hung on him, and he found himself taking deep breaths to steady his nerves. Occasionally, other individuals would pass through the waiting area, their presence briefly distracting David from his focused state. As time passed, his patience was tested. He found questions in the stillness of the waiting area, allowing himself to immerse in moments of introspection. He reflected on the purpose of his visit, contemplating the possible outcomes.

As David traced his fingers over the rough texture of the wall, he marvelled at the stories it seemed to hold. Some marks were deep as if someone had angrily scraped their nails against them, while others were faint, barely visible. David imagined the people who had left their marks, wondering what emotions had driven them to do so. He started to count them all. "Times by 10 is..." David continued to count the marks on the wall, his mind working to calculate the total. Concentrating deeply, he focused on multiplying the count by 1000, the numbers swirling in his head. Suddenly, a loud door slam reverberated through the corridor, jolting David out of his thoughts and causing his irritation to escalate. He instinctively covered his ears with his hands, seeking safety from the clamour. Feeling overwhelmed, David retreated to the corner adjacent to the office door, hoping to find some refuge from the disturbance.

From his hiding spot, David strained his ears, trying to make sense of the muffled voices emanating from the office. Despite his heightened sensitivity to sound, he managed to catch snippets of the conversation. Listening intently, he pieced together fragments of sentences and discerned different tones in their voices. The voices inside the office intrigued David, and his curiosity grew stronger. He strained to hear more, his focus sharpened as he absorbed every word and inflection. The snippets of conversation fuelled his imagination, igniting a desire to uncover the secrets being discussed behind that closed door. David's acute listening skills and his ability to decipher the subtleties in the voices would undoubtedly play a crucial role in what he discovered.

Mrs. Longane, the foster care coordinator, sat behind her desk, her expression reflected a sense of weariness. The defeated couple took their seats in front of her, their faces engraved with frustration and exhaustion. Mrs. Longane leaned forward, her voice toned with disappointment and concern, "You are the third set of foster parents who have taken care of David. I'm deeply worried that this will be a significant disruption for him."

The woman, desperate to convey her understanding and commitment, spoke up, "I'm truly sorry, Mrs. Longane, but we have genuinely tried our best to understand David's differences. We have been patient and supportive throughout."

The man, unable to contain his frustration any longer, added to the conversation, "But it's the violent outbursts that have become unbearable. David has punched holes in our walls, and he even physically struck out, nearly hitting my wife. We have reached a breaking point, and we can't endure this anymore."

The brutality of the situation lay fiercely as Mrs. Longane absorbed their words. The couple's plea for understanding, and their candid account of the challenges they had faced with David highlighted the complexity of the situation. It was clear that finding a suitable and stable environment for David would require time and thoughtful consideration. As the conversation unfolded between the foster parents and Mrs. Longane, David's acute hearing picked up on the dialogue. The reality of their words seemed to resonate deeply within him, causing a surge of emotions to well up inside. Feeling overwhelmed by the intensity of his thoughts, David instinctively slapped his head with both hands. The abrupt gesture was an expression of frustration and internal turmoil. It was as if he was trying to find a physical release for the emotions that swirled within him.

As his words continued, Dave's uneasiness grew, causing him to fidget nervously in his seat. In his agitation, he accidentally knocked over his tea, causing it to spill onto his clothes. A small gasp escaped his lips as he felt the warmth seep through. David glanced at Michelle, hoping for some assistance or acknowledgment of the mishap. However, Michelle appeared engrossed in her search for his file, unaware of the accident that had just occurred. Her focus remained solely on locating the necessary documents.

With a surge of frustration and disappointment, David realised that Michelle was too preoccupied to notice his predicament. He hesitated for a moment, unsure of how to proceed. The wetness of his clothes began to dampen his spirits, adding to the mounting discomfort he already felt.

Finally, as Michelle located the file she had been searching for, relief washed over her. Her eyes then caught sight of David's wet top, and amusement replaced the initial sense of accomplishment. Michelle's attention shifted from the file to David, her dominant instincts kicked in.

She joyfully realised the discomfort he must be experiencing and the impact it could have on their conversation, "Oh, David, I'm so sorry! I didn't notice the spill. Are you alright?"

David looked up at Michelle, his expression vulnerable and relieved. He nodded, grateful for her acknowledgment and concern.

"Let me grab some paper towels. We'll get you cleaned up right away." Sensing his embarrassment, Michelle quickly went in search of a towel. She returned moments later, holding a damp cloth in her hand. With a mischievous smile on her face, she walked over to Dave and started wiping his mouth and the top of his T-shirt, which had gotten a little messy. "Clumsy teddy bear," Michelle giggled, her eyes sparkling childishly.

Dave blushed and muttered, "Sorry."

Michelle chuckled and teasingly replied, "It's not me who is wet. Well, not yet anyway." Dave's face turned beet root red, and he coughed nervously, feeling even more self-conscious.

"I get the impression you've never really been taken care of?" Michelle said half-jokingly. Dave was mortified. He stared down at her deep red carpet in the dreadful silence, hoping to overcome his discomfort.

"Dave?" Michelle screeched, unimpressed by his expression of boredom, "have you always felt alone?" then continued, "Have you had to look after yourself?"

Her collective and eager questioning required a prompt response. Dave was worried his silence would jar her unscrupulous behaviour. He sat back, hoping to satisfy Michelle's inquest by detailing what felt like his pathetic life.

Three months ago, feeling a bit dishevelled Dave gathered himself after nearly stumbling over his own feet. He walked towards his house, which was four doors down from where the taxi dropped him off. As he approached the row of terraced houses, he took a few moments to look at the familiar surroundings. The terraced houses were quaint and neatly lined up along the street, each with its unique character. Some had small front gardens decorated with potted plants, while others had bicycles parked outside, indicating the presence of active residents.

Dave reached into his pocket and pulled out his house keys. As he did so, a tissue and a handful of small change fell out. He quickly bent down to retrieve the fallen items, knowing how important it was not to lose any money given his current situation. With a sigh of relief, he smiled happily, feeling a sense of ease as he prepared to enter his home. Walking closer to his house, his steps were a little unsteady due to his tiredness. He passed by three neighbouring houses until he reached his own.

The house had a front door painted in a faded shade of blue and a small window filled with cracks and mould. As he approached his door, he was greeted by two unexpected visitors.

"Hey?" Dave's voice wavered with uncertainty.

"Hi, Dave," responded a tall slim lady with a warm

smile. "My name is Lynsey, and this is Josh. We're from the crisis team."

Dave nodded, still unsure of what to make of their sudden presence. His mind began to wander. Anxiety draped over him.

Josh, with a concerned expression on his face, "You all right, Dave? Is it okay to come in and have a chat, mate?" he asked gently.

Dave hesitated for a moment before responding, "Err, yeah."

Before they entered, they could see a rundown front door. Its once vibrant colour had faded, and the peeling paint revealed the weathered wood beneath. The doorknob was slightly loose, and as he turned it, they could hear the aged mechanism creaking under his touch. The hinges squeaked in protest as the door swung open, revealing a glimpse of his world.

As they stepped inside, Lynsey and Josh discreetly covered their noses, trying not to make it obvious. The stench of faeces permeated the air, making it unbearable. Dave closed the door behind them and noticed their reaction. He quickly apologised, "Sorry about the smell, my toilet is blocked."

Lynsey tried to downplay the situation, politely suggesting, "Is that what it is?" She exchanged a concerned glance with Josh. Stepping through the doorway, they noticed the windows that lined the front of the house. They were smudged with dirt and grime, obscuring the view outside. The faded and tattered thin curtains hung limply, allowing only feeble rays of sunlight to enter into the room. The place looked extremely void of care and love and the scent that hung aggressively in the air hinted loudly at a lack of fresh air and proper cleaning.

They walked past the kitchen. The linoleum floor was scuffed and worn in places, and the cabinets showed signs of water damage. The smell of old food lingered, indicating dismal cleaning routines. Piles of unwashed dishes sat in the sink, and the refrigerator door was covered with sticky notes and expired grocery lists. Continuing down the hall they entered the lounge.

Dave gestured towards a room, "We can go in here. I'll shut the door, and it won't smell so bad." The room felt dim, with heavy curtains drawn shut which blocked out most of the natural light. The worn-out sofa, covered with a faded blanket, sagged in the middle and showed obvious signs of prolonged use. The coffee table was cluttered with scattered papers, empty coffee cups, and neglected magazines. Dust settled heavily on the surfaces, which further highlighted the lack of attention given to the room's upkeep.

The room was heavy with unspoken tension as Lynsey finally addressed Dave, inquiring about his well-being. Dave, with a heavy sigh, disclosed his struggles with his IBS. Josh then attempted to redirect the conversation, asking Dave about his feelings regarding the previous night event. Dave's responses were guarded and defensive, revealing little about his inner turmoil.

Lynsey and Josh clarified their purpose in visiting Dave daily, emphasising their commitment to providing support and preventing further self-harm. Despite their efforts to engage with Dave, his demeanour remained distant and despondent. Dave's words echoed a deep sense of hopelessness, expressing a desire for an end to his suffering.

Josh, adopting a more empathetic tone, encouraged Dave to open up about his pain, offering to explore ways to improve his quality of life. However, Dave's bleak response hinted at the magnitude of his despair, leaving his companions grasping for a way to help him find a glimmer of hope in the darkness that enveloped him.

Lynsey's intervention was met with a sense of resignation from Dave, who expressed his disillusionment with past attempts to seek help. Josh, recognising the importance of understanding Dave's current treatment, inquired about his medication with a gentle tone, ready to document the details.

Seated on his worn-out couch, Dave's weary countenance mirrored his emotional exhaustion and despair. The weight of the conversation lingered in the room as Josh addressed Dave's medication regimen, specifically mentioning sertraline. Dave, overcome with fatigue, acknowledged that he needed rest, his voice barely above a whisper.

Sensing the gravity of the situation, Lynsey approached Dave with empathy, offering a lifeline of support. She reassured him and handed him a card with the crisis team's contact information, urging him to reach out if he found himself in distress again. Josh stood by, a silent but supportive presence, as they collectively sought to provide Dave with a sense of comfort and a reminder that he was not alone in his struggles.

Dave accepted the card with trembling hands, his emotions swirling beneath the surface. He managed a strained "Yeah," his voice laden with unspoken turmoil.

Josh interjected, offering a semblance of comfort and commitment to their continued support. With a professional yet friendly tone, he assured Dave of their visit the following day, his gaze unwavering.

Dave nodded again, impatiently this time. "Yeah. Okay, bye," he fought to say, hoping this was his last goodbye. As Dave closed the front door, he felt exasperated by their visit. He stood there for a few minutes, leaning against the door, focusing on his depressing home. It always felt strangely quiet, but at that moment, it felt like he was living outside of his body, as if he were a third person observing himself in his home.

Dave was suddenly hit with the rank smell of an overflowed shitty loo. He walked to his downstairs bathroom which was at the back of the house. He stood there for a few minutes, gawked with disgust at the sight of his toilet, jammed with diarrhoea and toilet paper. The bathroom had been transformed into a chaotic scene. Toilet paper rolls were tossed aside in a frenzy, landing haphazardly on the floor. The smell filled the air, making it difficult for Dave to breathe. He clung to the toilet sink for dear life as wave after wave of diarrhoea overtook him. Dave battled against the stubborn clog, his efforts only seemed to exacerbate the situation. With each forceful plunge, the toilet gushed forth with an explosive eruption of diarrhoea, splattering the bathroom walls in an absurd and grotesque display. The more Dave tried to clean up the mess, the messier it became, engulfing the entire bathroom in an unholy symphony of filth. He ruminated for a while, deliberating what to do. He leaned back against the bathroom wall, then slithered down until he reached the floor. Dave fecklessly put his head into his wide hands. Raw and ageing suicide scars were discernible. Still in the same position, he slowly lifted his head, his eyes slothfully scanning the bathroom.

His eyes wandered to the light switch cord hanging from the ceiling. The additional piece of string, knotted and fragile, represented a lifeline, a glimmer of hope within his darkness. It dangled there as if waiting for him to make a choice. His gaze shifted to the razor, its worn appearance reflected the battles he had fought. The blade gleamed with a dangerous temptation that whispered promises of escape from his torment. He observed the scars on his arms, which served as a haunting reminder of previous suicide attempts, marking the depths of his despair.

Dave picked up the bin and emptied the contents. Grubby old tissues, drained toothpaste tubes and empty shampoo bottles crashed onto the floor. He removed the plastic bin bag and put it over his head and he tied a knot so that he had no air to breathe. He started to suffocate and became hysterical. He clenched his fists, determined not to rip the bag off his head. The suction of the bag into his mouth caused extreme palpitations, his body started to tremble. Within seconds, he abruptly ripped the bag off his head. He froze with shock, then suddenly laughed, his screams of laughter grew louder as he squinted at all the splattered defecation sprawled in front of him. Trying to control his strained amusement, he knelt over his toilet and peered down. He voraciously used his hand to pick up all the piled excrement.

Bit by bit he quickly gripped as much shit as possible and put it into the plastic bin bag. He did this several times, gathering all the turds which managed to gush between his fingers, back into the toilet. Dave became distracted by the sound of flapping paper.

In a sudden flash, he realised where he was and reverted to reality where Michelle anxiously waved a stack of printed papers in the air.

"Dave? Dave?" Michelle exclaimed, her voice filled with urgency.

Startled, Dave turned his attention towards Michelle and replied, "Yeah? What?"

He glanced around the office, trying to make sense of the situation. Irritation crept into his expression as he looked back at Michelle.

A patronising grin spread across Michelle's face. "Are you sure about that?" she burst into laughter, her amusement pinging through the office. Playfully, she handed him a pen and pointed to a spot on the papers.

"Please sign there," Michelle said, still chuckling at her own joke.

Dave's eyes sank with disbelief, "I'm fine. Thanks."

Michelle raised an eyebrow, her rejection evident, "Are you though, Dave?"

Dave paused, contemplating Michelle's question. He finally saw through her facade.

He looked carefully at Michelle, felt perplexed and

then with a sudden win, he wondered if her erratic questioning was a deflection of her own pain and trauma. He speedily made a silent promise to not overthink this unusual encounter, his priority was to return to Claire, where he felt safe.

"Michelle, seriously? I know I can be a bit slow sometimes, but come on," Dave retorted, his annoyance clearly showed.

Michelle sighed in disbelief, she chose to ignore his effort to stand up for himself.

Dave begrudgingly took the pen and signed the papers.

He stood up, ready to escape the uncomfortable situation. With disdain and sarcasm, Dave asked, "Am I allowed to leave now?"

Michelle chuckled good-naturedly, blending politeness with a hint of playfulness. "Well, of course. I'll call Chloe to escort you back, just so you don't get lost."

Shortly after, Dave strolled down the corridors with Chloe by his side, guiding him to Claire's room, where he intended to go. Upon arriving, Dave broke the silence with a simple "Thanks."

Chloe responded with a warm smile, expressing her

pleasure in assisting him. Dave nodded gratefully, acknowledging her help. With that, Chloe left him for the evening, leaving Dave to carry on with his visit to Claire.

Chloe approached Marcus and Kay's door and knocked firmly yet quietly. Kay opened the door, greeting Chloe with a worried smile. Chloe responded with a smile of her own and informed Kay about Marcus's assessment with Michelle being ready. She offered to take him down, seeking Kay's approval.

After a moment of consideration, Kay inquired if she could accompany them. Chloe hesitated briefly before agreeing to Kay's request. Kay expressed her excitement at being included, and she requested a few minutes to prepare before closing the door, leaving Chloe waiting outside for their departure.

CHAPTER 16

~MICHELLE'S FLASHBACK~

Seated at her desk, Michelle felt her heart race and a surge of anxiety wash over her. The presence of the two imposing men in designer suits standing before her, staring at her with an intimidating stance, heightened her nervousness. Despite her trepidation, she discreetly took a breath to compose herself and maintained a professional demeanour. Greeting the guests arrogantly, Michelle said, "Good morning, gentlemen. How may I assist you today?" She stood up, walked confidently towards the two men, and exuded a mixture of fear and determination. Michelle had made a promise, and now her credibility hung in the balance.

Michelle confidently asserted that she had agreed to resolve everything by the week's end, maintaining eye contact with the sceptical Man A. Despite her assertion, Man A remained unconvinced, crossing his arms and expressing distrust, citing previous unfulfilled promises. Michelle, feeling her patience wane, understood the stakes but refused to succumb to fear. Stepping forward, she challenged Man B directly, displaying defiance in her voice, offering the choice to either trust her or take whatever action they deemed necessary. Feeling the pressure of the situation, Man B impatiently interrupted, emphasising the seriousness of the impending deadline and the dire consequences if they did not receive the payments as promised by the end of the week.

Michelle made a sarcastic remark, suggesting that they could kill her immediately. Man B interjected with impatience, fully aware of the severity of the situation at hand. He scolded Michelle, emphasising that it was not the appropriate moment for joking or acting clever. Man B warned her that failing to deliver the payments by the end of the week would result in consequences far worse than just losing her life.

Michelle understood the dire consequences that awaited her if she failed to deliver. She watched the two men exchange a knowing glance, a silent agreement passing between them.

Michelle, distracting her stressful thoughts, inquired

about the demand for organs and whether they were sold on the black market discreetly? She chuckled at the idea, boldly announcing in a song-like tone, that kidneys, brains and hearts were available for sale to the highest bidder, advising anyone in need of a new heart to have significant funds for the purchase.

The man asked about the reason for her questions and statements. Michelle defended herself, stating that showing interest in her inventory wasn't a crime. The man redirected her queries to the boss. Michelle sarcastically mentioned the boss, referring to him as her supposed father. The men exchanged glances. Michelle speculated that it wouldn't be surprising if he was responsible for her mother's murder and the illicit harvesting of her organs. This revelation made the men visibly uncomfortable. The last thing they wanted was to be part of some family drama.

Man A finally spoke, his voice cold and resolute. "We'll be back," he said ominously, leaving no room for doubt. As they turned to leave, Michelle felt the dread enveloping her. She had one week to fulfil her promise and salvage her life. Failure was not an option, for the consequences would be far greater than she could bear.

With renewed determination, Michelle resolved to do whatever it took to make things right. Time was running out, and she could only hope that her word would finally be trusted, and her actions would speak louder than any lingering doubt.

CHAPTER 17

~MICHELLE & MARCUS and KAY~

M ichelle nervously stood by the door as Chloe escorted Marcus and Kay into the room. Chloe departed, leaving Michelle alone with the visitors. "Come in," Michelle ordered, her voice slightly unhinged. "Hello, can I get you both a drink?" she asked, trying to break the tension.

Kay glanced at Marcus before replying, "No, thanks. We've just had one."

Michelle gestured for Kay to take a seat and settled herself into her chair.

As Kay sat, her eyes gravitated towards the poster hanging on the stand next to Michelle's desk that had already caught the eyes of many clients.

"We don't like to see anyone suffer. We want to help the best we can," Michelle said, her voice becoming less sincere. She opened Marcus's file, preparing herself for the conversation ahead.

"I'm really sorry about your accident, Marcus. It's very unfortunate," Michelle continued, with a forced tone of sincerity.

Kay looked at Marcus, her eyes welling with sympathy. "It all happened so quickly," Kay said with deep sadness before continuing, "One minute, we were having a family breakfast together, then next... well, everything changed."

Michelle nodded understandingly, acknowledging the suddenness of the tragedy.

"Some of us are just unlucky, aren't we?" Michelle remarked, which sounded superficial with a touch of melancholy.

Kay's eyes shot to Michelle, her expression reflected confusion and frustration.

"It was a fall, right?" Michelle asked, trying to gather more information and develop a better understanding of the circumstances surrounding Marcus's accident.

Kay's voice crackled slightly as she reminisced about happier times. "Yes," she replied, with a hint of nostalgia in her tone as she explained, "He used to be so full of energy. So much fun. He always made me laugh." A bittersweet smile crept onto Kay's face as she recalled the moments they had shared, the joy and laughter that used to fill their lives. The weight of the present situation pressed heavily upon her, contrasting sharply with the vibrant memories of the past ...

In the heart of a quaint, cosy neighbourhood, nestled within a well-kept family home, lived a remarkable working-class family. They were the epitome of contentment, radiating warmth and kindness wherever they went. Marcus, a gentle soul, and his adoring wife Kay created a haven of love and tranquillity. As their love deepened, they desperately wanted a child. After years of trying, they felt such gratitude when Arlo was born. He had grown up to be a polite and respectful young boy who worshipped his mum and dad which was a testament to the nurturing environment created by two loving, positive role models.

One bright morning, as the first rays of sunlight filtered through the kitchen window, Marcus stepped into the kitchen. His heart brimming with affection, he approached Kay who stood by the stove skilfully frying eggs and sausages for their breakfast. As he gently wrapped his arms around her waist, Marcus planted a tender kiss on the nape of her neck, filling the room with an aura of tenderness.

Kay turned to face him; her eyes twinkled with joy as she met Marcus' adoring gaze. The sizzle of the cooking food filtered through the air, harmonising with the palpable love surrounding the room. Marcus couldn't help but beam with delight as he beheld the delicious spread before them. Their cosy kitchen became a sanctuary of love, where the delightful smell of sizzling sausages and the crackle of frying eggs mingled with the laughter and affection shared by Marcus and Kay. It was these simple moments that they found the most endearing, their love growing stronger with each passing day.

Marcus caught a whiff of the aroma from the food. "That smells delicious," he delightfully expressed, his mouth watering.

Playfully, Kay pushed him away with a smile, "Move then, so I can get it ready."

Just then, their energetic and happy son, Arlo, who was thirteen years old, strolled into the kitchen. Arlo's eyes lit up as he saw the spread of sausages, eggs, toast, and beans on the kitchen counter. "Yes, I'm starving," he claimed eagerly. Kay, feeling a bit flustered, started placing the food onto three plates that were waiting on the kitchen unit. Once the plates were ready, Kay carried them over to the dining table. Arlo beamed at his mum's cooking and remarked, "Mum... you're the best!"

Kay's face lit up with delight as she replied, "Well, enjoy."

Without wasting any time, they all dug into their hearty breakfast. After a few bites, Marcus turned to Kay and said, "This is really nice. Thank you, baby."

Kay smiled but had a sneaky idea. "Well, since you both like it so much, you won't mind doing the dishes, right?" she joked with some seriousness.

Marcus, trying to deflect, replied, "I'm sure Arlo won't mind doing them on his own."

Arlo chimed in, "Nah, I'll let you do 'em instead, Dad."

Marcus, attempting to steal one of Arlo's sausages, was swiftly pushed away. Arlo grinned and said, "Yeah, I don't think so."

Hearing the playful banter, Kay intervened and jokingly advised, "Be kind, son, sharing is caring remember."

But Arlo, still munching on his food, looked at his dad and cleverly retorted, "Your turn to be kind, so it's your turn to do the dishes, Dad."

Kay, trying to keep the peace, suggested, "Let's just eat our breakfast, and then you can sort out who's doing them."

Marcus, wanting to change the subject, asked Arlo, "Are you ready for tomorrow's match?" Arlo nodded enthusiastically, "Yeah, hopefully we can thrash the other team. They're from West High, so they need putting down."

Kay reminded her son, "Close your mouth when you're eating, Arlo."

Marcus rejoined the conversation, "Are you still playing midfielder?"

Arlo confidently affirmed, "Of course. You're still coming, right Dad?"

"Sure, when have I ever missed a game?"

They exchanged a high five, filled with excitement for the upcoming match.

As they savoured the last bites of their breakfast, their morning banter continued, bringing warmth and joy to their family table. Marcus felt full and energised after their delicious breakfast. He got up from the table, looked at Arlo, then at the dirty plates, and with a mischievous grin he pushed his plate towards Arlo. Playfully, Arlo jumped up from his seat and dashed towards the stairs, knowing that his dad would give chase.

Marcus quickly followed, their laughter filling the house as they engaged in their usual game of chase. Meanwhile, Kay rolled her eyes at their antics but couldn't help her smile. She sighed, still holding her plate with the last few bites of her breakfast. Glancing at the dirty dishes on the table, she shook her head in amusement. Despite the mess, she found herself feeling grateful for these silly moments with her family.

As she continued to eat, Kay listened to the sound of her husband and son's laughter echoing through the house. Their playful silliness warmed her heart and brought a sense of contentment. She chuckled softly, knowing that even though they could be a handful, moments like these were what made their family bond strong and cherished.

Arlo's shouted excitement grew louder as he realised he had almost reached the stairs. He could feel the rush of accomplishment and anticipation building within him. Looking back, he saw his dad not far behind, which encouraged him to keep going. Arlo's determination intensified, and he let out a triumphant roar, a mix of excitement and a playful challenge to his dad.

With each step, Arlo's foot hit the ground with purpose and competitiveness. He could almost taste victory as his goal of conquering the stairs drew nearer. The sound of his dad's footsteps pounded behind him, providing an extra boost of motivation.

As Arlo almost reached the top of the step, a surge of exhilaration washed over him. While cheering with excitement about beating his dad, Marcus tried to grab his ankle. Arlo managed to escape Marcus's firm grip and retaliated by kicking back and hitting Marcus's nose. Marcus let out a howl of pain due to the unexpected force of the impact which caused Marcus to fall back. As he landed back onto the floor, a dreadful sound of bones snapping repeated in Arlo's ears, haunting him.

In the aftermath of the accident, Arlo's mind raced as he comprehended the gravity of the situation. He stood frozen, his eyes wide with shock and disbelief. Panic surged through him as he realised the potential severity of his actions. He ran back down the stairs where he was faced with his lifeless dad. His hands were shaking uncontrollably as he reached out to his father, his voice choked with fear.

"Dad? Dad? Are you okay?" Arlo's voice quivered, his heart pounding in his chest. But there was no response. Marcus lay motionless on the floor, his body contorted in an unnatural position. After hearing the commotion, Kay rushed towards them. She looked down to Marcus, and her heart dropped with fear. Panic filled her eyes as she knelt beside him, desperately hoping he would wake up.

"Marcus, Marcus? Wake up!" she cried out, her voice trembling with pain. Beside her, Arlo still stood frozen, his face pale and frightened. The room began to fill with eerie silence, broken only by the sound of Arlo's racing heartbeat.

"Call an ambulance, quick!" Kay urgently instructed Arlo, her voice laced with desperation. Time was of the essence; they needed medical help right away.

Feeling for Marcus's pulse, Kay's hands shook uncontrollably. She tried to remain calm for his sake, reassuring him softly. Her touch was gentle as she stroked his head, fighting back tears that threatened to escape. But deep down, she couldn't help but feel a sense of panic.

Arlo snapped out of his shock, realising the seriousness of the situation. He hurried into the lounge and grabbed the phone where he dialled for an ambulance. However, his trembling hands betrayed him, causing the phone to slip from his grasp and fall to the ground.

Undeterred, Kay continued to comfort Marcus, trying to convey hope and constant reassurance. She did everything in her power to keep him stable, desperately clinging to the belief that help would arrive anytime soon. Meanwhile, Arlo managed to regain himself and quickly prepared for effective communication with the emergency services.

His voice quivered as he spoke into the phone, relaying the dire situation, "Ambulance, please. It's my dad. He fell down the stairs and he's unconscious." He provided the necessary details, the address of their home in Saxon Gardens, New Fields, and begged for a swift response.

As he hung up the phone, Arlo relayed the instructions he had received, "They said not to move him and to make him comfortable." They had to do everything they could until help arrived, and they clung to the hope that the ambulance would be there soon. In the tense atmosphere of a silent house, Arlo's fear and distress intensified as he waited for the ambulance. He felt a surge of helplessness, unsure of what to do to alleviate the situation. His eyes shifted between his dad and mum, overwhelmed.

Kay, too upset to speak, sought solace by placing her head next to Marcus's, desperately wanting to seek comfort and hope in their shared presence. The silence in the house only amplified her nerves, and she found herself yearning for the sound of sirens, hoping that the arrival of the ambulance would bring some relief.

Kay and her son Arlo sat in the visitors area surrounded by other waiting people. Arlo, a restless boy, couldn't sit still and began shaking his legs from side to side. His constant movement caught Kay's attention, and she started to feel agitated, perhaps due to the combination of Arlo's restlessness and the anticipation of whatever they were waiting for.

Kay reached for her mobile phone and checked it, likely hoping to distract herself or find something to occupy her mind. She scrolled through messages, emails, or social media updates, trying to divert her attention from the situation at hand. However, her agitation persisted, and she found it difficult to focus on her phone amidst the restlessness in the room. Kay thought about engaging with Arlo in a conversation to minimise his fidgeting, but she struggled to find any words to speak.

Kay and Arlo exchanged a short glance, trying to offer each other small gestures of support and understanding. Kay really wanted to reassure Arlo, to inform him that their wait would soon be over and they would be on their way. Despite her wishes, Kay was struggling too much, trying to make sense of this awful situation. She didn't have the strength to provide comfort; she was filled with too much uncertainty. Kay's and Arlo's heads both immediately turned to the door which was opened by a doctor, Mr. Lowry. He approached Kay with a grave expression on his face. "Mrs. Adams?" the doctor addressed her.

Kay nodded, her face was filled with worry. "Yes, how is he?"

The doctor gestured towards a nearby meeting room, "Can we go somewhere a bit quieter to talk?" Kay nodded again, her heartbeat multiplied in her chest. Together, they walked towards the meeting room.

Mr. Lowry cleared his throat before speaking and Kay felt a wave of apprehension wash over her. She nodded in response, her heart pounding in her chest as she followed him down the hallway. Each step felt heavy with anticipation, the silence between them thick with unspoken words.

Kay's heart raced as they entered the small meeting room. The doctor, Mr. Lowry, took a seat across from her, his expression still solemn. Kay sat down, her hands trembling in her lap as she waited for the news about her husband.

The room seemed to close in around them, the weight of the moment palpable in the air. Kay's mind raced with a million questions, each one more daunting than the last. She searched the doctor's face for any hint of what was to come, but his features remained stoic and inscrutable.

A heavy silence settled over the room as Mr. Lowry gathered his thoughts, the tension mounting with each passing second. Kay braced herself for the inevitable, hoping to resolve whatever lay ahead.

At that moment, as the doctor prepared to speak, time seemed to stand still. The unspoken words hung in the air like a storm on the horizon, ready to break and change everything in their wake. Kay took a deep breath, her gaze steady and her spirit unyielding, as she waited for the truth to be revealed.

Mr. Lowry watched the storm of emotions swirling inside her. Arlo's eyes welled up with tears as he waited alongside his mother.

The doctor's sombre expression mirrored the gravity of the situation as he spoke, his voice filled with regret, "I'm sorry, Mrs. Adams. The injuries your husband sustained are severe. I'm afraid that he will ever walk again."

A shiver ran down Kay's spine as she tried to process the harsh reality of their new life ahead.

Tears streamed down Kay's cheeks as she whispered, her voice trembling, "What... what can we do?"

The doctor's gaze softened, his empathy was shared as he replied, "We will do everything we can to support Marcus in his recovery and rehabilitation. It will be a long and difficult road ahead, but with the right care and determination, there is hope for improvement."

Kay nodded, her mind swirling with a whirlwind of emotions. She reached out and took Arlo's hand, their bond a lifeline in the midst of chaos. Together, they braced themselves for the challenges that lay ahead, united in their love and determination to navigate this new chapter of their lives.

As Kay sat traumatised, the doctor gave her a moment to collect herself. "What now?" Holding back tears, she sought desperately for guidance amongst the chaos that had engulfed her mind.

The doctor detailed the devastation. He explained that Marcus had suffered severe injuries to his first and second cervical vertebrae, resulting in damage to his spinal cord.

Kay couldn't understand how such a horrific accident could occur while her husband was merely chasing their son up the stairs engaged in innocent play. Seeking confirmation, she turned to Arlo, who tearfully affirmed her words.

Kay felt confused about how something so unimaginable happened in an instant? Trying to provide answers amidst the despair, the doctor shared a small bridge of hope. He assured Kay that while her husband would require a ventilator to breathe, there was no brain damage. Although this was a small relief, it hardly lessened the severity of the situation for Kay.

Feeling the heavy load of responsibility, Kay inquired about the care her husband would need. The doctor explained that once Marcus regained enough strength, he would be referred to a rehabilitation centre. There, he would embark on a journey of learning new skills, such as operating an electric wheelchair and adapting to a life supported by the ventilator. As the doctor paused, he tried to empathise with the immense shock and grief they were experiencing. He reassured them both that the medical staff would do everything possible to assist and support their family during this difficult time.

Kay's mind was flooded with an array of emotions — sadness, worry, and uncertainty, but also a flicker of determination. She knew that their lives had been irrevocably changed, but she would always be there for her husband, no matter what, to provide the love and care he would need in the days ahead.

The doctor posed a question that caught Kay off guard. "Would you like to see him?" he asked, his voice gentle yet direct.

Kay's heart skipped a beat, and she looked at the doctor with feelings of worry and anticipation. With a hesitant nod, Kay agreed to see him. Her hands trembled, mirroring the uneasiness that gripped her.

As they approached the room, Kay's heart pounded in her chest. She clung tightly to Arlo's hand, drawing strength from his presence. They entered the room, and there he was, lying still on the bed, his face pale and vulnerable. Kay stood at the doorway, her heart heavy with emotion as she looked at Marcus unconscious on the hospital bed. The sight of him hooked up to various machines, including the ventilator tube in his mouth, was both surreal and devastating. She fought back tears, feeling a mix of fear, helplessness, and deep sadness. As she tried to calm herself, Kay's attention was momentarily diverted as Arlo ran off. Concerned for him, she contemplated chasing after him but hesitated, torn between her desire to comfort Arlo and her longing to be by Marcus's side.

Stepping back into the room, Kay approached Marcus's bedside, her eyes blinded by his motionless form. She reached out her unsteady hand and slowly placed it on his, feeling the warmth of his skin despite the sterile environment. Memories of their time together flooded her mind, and the moments of their shared experiences intensified her grief. Kay leaned in closer, her voice felt trapped in a dream, as she spoke to Marcus.

She told him how much he meant to her, how his presence had brought joy and love into her life. She shared her hopes for his recovery, promising to stay by his side and support him through whatever lay ahead. She started to sob, tears streaming down her face, but she found relief in the fact that Marcus couldn't see her pain.

With a heavy heart, Kay took a deep breath and forced herself to step away from Marcus's bedside. She knew that she needed to find Arlo, to provide comfort and reassurance to him, as well. As she walked towards the door, she glanced back one last time; she silently promised Marcus that she would return soon.

Leaving the intensive care unit, Kay felt lost and overwhelmed with pain. In order to forget and distract her immense emotions, she set out to find Arlo, hoping to offer him the help they both needed in this difficult time.

Next day

Kay sat close to Marcus, hoping he would wake up soon. She felt at ease when a friendly nurse entered the room, carrying tubes and wipes. She smiled back politely, acknowledging the nurse's presence, and then returned her attention to Marcus, who was peacefully asleep. The nurse approached the bed, setting the tubes and wipes on a nearby tray.

She checked the monitors and machines, ensuring everything was functioning properly.

Kay watched the nurse work quietly, appreciating the care and attention given to Marcus. She knew the nurses would now play a vital role in his recovery, monitoring his condition and providing the necessary medical support. She stroked his hair gently, sending her love and support through the connection. Despite the difficulties they faced, she found some courage in knowing that a dedicated team of healthcare professionals was working hard to help Marcus regain his health.

The nurse informed Kay that she needed to open his bowels.

Kay looked puzzled, "You mean the toilet?"

The nurse nodded, "Yes, but in order for him to do that, I'll need to remove his catheter." Understanding the procedure, Kay asked, "Is this a regular thing?" The nurse explained, "Yes, this will need to be done every couple of days to prevent any blockages."

Kay's concern deepened as she asked, "Will I have to do this when he comes home?" Reassuringly, the nurse advised Kay that she was sure a nurse would visit her at home to assist with some of his daily needs.

Kay sighed with relief, informing the nurse she was waiting to discuss home care options.

The nurse suggested that she thought it would be useful for her to learn the procedure, just in case.

Kay revealed. "But I won't have the time due to work and other commitments."

"Don't worry, it shouldn't take long." Taking a deep breath, the nurse lifted the sheets, struggling to lift Marcus's legs. Kay stepped in to help. The nurse placed a small towel on Marcus's groin area.

"Firstly," the nurse began explaining, "We have to deflate the balloon and take the catheter out."

Carefully, the nurse carried out the procedure while Kay observed. As the nurse pulled the tube free, a small amount of urine dribbled out, which the nurse quickly wiped away with the towel.

"Now," the nurse continued, "We need to massage his abdomen, pressing hard and moving from right to left." Kay watched the nurse demonstrate the technique, "This will help move the stool along and eventually out. It usually only takes a few minutes, but sometimes it can take a lot longer."

Feeling bewildered, Kay expressed her need for some fresh air. She rushed out of the room, where she started off walking slowly and then out of nowhere, she sprinted away erratically, searching for a safe space or a moment where she could escape her present predicament, and calmly collect her thoughts and emotions. Running down the corridors without a clue where to go, she turned left then right, trying to avoid crowds of people in the corridor, who were perplexed by her urgency. She noticed the ladies toilets and made a prompt entrance. Kay looked into a large mirror which hung on top of the toilet wash basins. As she stared frozen at her reflection, she noticed the heaviness in her breathing.

Recognising the need to regain control, she took a few slow deep breaths, attempting to steady herself. She reached to the taps for water and splashed some onto her face, feeling the coolness against her skin. The sensation helped to bring her focus back to the present moment. With each passing breath, Kay felt a gradual shift in her state of mind. The dabbled water on her face served as a physical reminder of her intention to regain control and find inner peace. As she continued to focus on her breathing and to make a conscious effort to calm herself, she began to feel self-control returning.

Through this process, Kay acknowledged her unsteady emotions and smartly took proactive steps to manage them. She understood that self-control was a skill that could be cultivated with practice and patience. With renewed composure, she prepared to face whatever challenges lay ahead, feeling more centred and grounded in that moment.

She made her way back towards Marcus, with her silent footsteps, she felt more at ease now that she had built up the strength to be able to support his needs. Kay worked hard trying to switch off her chaotic mind, and she eventually achieved this by focusing on the future as opposed to what happened and what she lost. Kay entered the room, relieved the nurse had left, so that she avoided any awkward questions and instructions. She needed to take one step at a time to be mentally prepared at the pace she felt comfortable with.

Sometime later, Arlo walked into the room, greeting his mother and father softly, trying not to disturb his father's rest. Kay greeted him with weariness and concern in her tone. Earlier that morning, the doctor had informed Kay that he had managed to talk to Marcus while he was awake and delivered some news during the night that left Marcus upset and unsure of how to process it all. Kay was uncertain how Marcus would react when he woke up, and she didn't want it to upset Arlo.

Arlo walked over to his mother's side and hugged her tightly. He offered, "Would you like a coffee or something? I can go get it for you, Mum." Kay smiled appreciatively at her son's thoughtfulness. "I'll have a coffee, please. Thank you, Arlo." He left the room in search of a coffee maker.

Not long after, Marcus stirred. His eyes flickered, and he gasped for air, before catching his breath through the ventilator as he recaptured his new reality. Kay reached out and gently straightened the crumpled sheet covering Marcus. She desperately wanted to find the right words to comfort him, to let him know that he wasn't alone in this difficult time. Marcus laid still in the hospital bed, his face was inscribed with worry.

"The doctor said he explained everything early this morning," confirming what he was already told. She searched in Marcus's eyes, hoping to find some understanding amidst the confusion.

Marcus remained silent, his mind flooded with a whirlwind of questions. He knew that his life was about to change in ways he couldn't comprehend, and the weight of it all was too overwhelming. In that moment, as Kay stood by his side, he looked at her with sorrow.

As if sensing his thoughts, Kay continued, her voice steady and filled with sincerity, "We're here for you, no matter what. We'll face this together, one step at a time."

In that brief exchange, Marcus was grateful, but it didn't make a difference to how he felt. He realised that he didn't want her to deal with such a burden. As that's what he now considered himself to be.

CHAPTER 18

~THE EXPLORATION~

L ater in the evening, Dave and Claire left their rooms to sneak downstairs into the kitchen/ dining area like disobedient schoolchildren. The place appeared to be deserted with no one in sight. As they made their way to the dining area, they leaned over the small counter, hoping to find someone who could help them.

"Hello?" Dave called out to the empty room. "We only want a coffee! Ok, just tea then?" His voice echoed, but there was no response.

"Everyone's disappeared," Claire observed, a hint of merry in her words.

Dave, always ready with his dark sense of humour, chipped in, "Perhaps they're all dead?"

Claire glanced at him, her eyes widening slightly, "Maybe the dead killed them?"

In a playful moment, Dave decided to go along. He quickly jumped behind Claire and began pretending to be a zombie, making eerie noises. Claire rolled her eyes at his antics.

"Freak," she muttered loudly, then suggested, "Let's go outside. I fancy a fag."

Dave happily agreed with her, "For once you talk sense."

As they opened the back exit doors and made their way to the picnic bench, a sense of relaxation washed over them. The cool breeze brushed against their skin as they settled down on a bench, enjoying the tranquillity of the communal garden. The garden, fenced off from the restricted area, offered a peaceful secluded spot away from thinking about tomorrow. If only they knew what awaited them beyond those fences,

With a flick of a lighter, they lit up their cigarettes, and they filled the air with a fragrant smoke. As they took a drag, the familiar warmth and flavour deepened their senses, adding to the moment of serenity. The conversation flowed effortlessly between them as they shared stories, thoughts, and laughter, enjoying the simple pleasure of each other's company.

There was a special moment of a powerful connection between them, an unfamiliar but uplifting experience for both. It was a pivotal moment where Claire and Dave finally felt seen, heard, and appreciated. A meaningful relationship developed that went far beyond superficial interactions, which was previously all that they'd ever encountered. Finding genuine human connection was a fundamental aspect of their lives that had always been missing.

"We need to smoke these before our number is called," Dave declared roguishly, holding up the pack of fags for Claire to see.

"That won't be hard," she declared with a hint of scepticism.

Dave's eyes twinkled with excitement as he glanced towards a nearby restricted area, surrounded by a tall fence. "The restricted area looks inviting," he announced defiantly. Claire's eyes widened in surprise, "So what? Ya gonna break in?"

Dave smirked mischievously, his mind already crafting a plan, "Why not? A little adventure never hurts anyone, right? I just wanna know what's there," Dave murmured.

Caught off guard by Dave's audacious statement, Claire arched an eyebrow and replied, "You mean you wanna find dead bodies? Are you out of your mind?"

Claire's instincts urged her to retreat to the safety of their rooms, but she couldn't deny the spark of curiosity that danced within her. "Maybe we should go back to our rooms and forget about this foolishness," she sounded slightly worried.

A rebellious spark ignited within Dave's soul. "You're scared of taking risks? Me, too!" he declared, his voice ignited with strength, "But fuck it, we'll be dead tomorrow anyway, so what's the worst they can do?"

Claire's eyes widened in shock at Dave's blunt proclamation. "Arrest us and then have us spend what remains of our depressing lives in prison."

With a conviction that bordered on madness, Dave leaned in closer to Claire, his voice swiftly lowered into a whisper, "They wouldn't have us arrested. We are patients here, and we're suicidal, aren't we?"

Silence broke as Claire absorbed Dave's words. She realised that their shared desperation for a taste of freedom had clouded their judgement. "I need another drink. Come on, let's go and finish the vodka." Claire uttered, trying to encourage Dave's need for spontaneity.

Dave, fuelled by a newfound sense of purpose, reached out and gently grasped Claire's soft hand. "We will," he assured her, with confidence and determination, "just as soon as we do one last stupid thing."

Dave took a final drag of his cigarette, savouring the last bit of smoke before extinguishing it with his trainer. With a sense of urgency, he walked over to the nearest picnic bench and dragged it towards the 6-foot fencing area. He positioned the bench next to the fence, creating a makeshift platform to help him reach higher. As Dave climbed up onto the picnic bench, he felt a surge of excitement. The wind rustled through his hair as he gazed at the fence in front of him. Without hesitation, he took a few steps back to gather momentum, and propelled himself forward with all his might. In a split second, his body soared through the air, defying gravity.

As Dave stretched his limbs, time seemed to slow down. He could feel the adrenaline coursing through his veins. His heart pounded in his chest. The world blurred around him as he cleared the fence effortlessly, his body sailing through the open space. For a brief moment, Dave felt weightless—a sense of freedom and liberation exploded inside him.

The ground approached rapidly, and he prepared himself for the landing. With a controlled descent, he touched down gracefully. His legs absorbed the impact, and he rolled forward, as he came to a stop with a triumphant smile on his face. Dave stood up straight, brushing off the dirt from his clothes, and looked back at the fence he just cleared. A sense of accomplishment made him feel proud. He took a leap of faith, defying the boundaries that confined him. In that daring moment, he embraced the thrill of adventure, reminding himself that life is full of opportunities to challenge and overcome barriers.

Claire's eyes blinked with surprise and worry. "What the fuck?" she mouthed. "You are actually mentally ill!"

Dave, seemingly unfazed by her outburst, grinned excitedly, "That's why we make a good team," he replied. "Now jump over and come with me," he called, encouraging Claire to join him on his defiant adventure. Claire took a deep drag from her cigarette, exhaling a plume of smoke before stubbing it out forcefully. She looked at the top of the fence with apprehension, her mind raced with thoughts of potential danger. "What?

And break my leg, or even worse, my neck," she moaned, as a sudden wave of anxiety took over her.

Dave softened, "I'll catch you, Claire. I promise. You have to trust me. I've spent my life thinking the worst, now's our only chance to do something where we don't have to try to feel safe."

Claire was confused by his statement and contemplated his proposal. She knew deep down that it was risky, but the allure of breaking rules and exploring the forbidden was undeniably tempting. Reluctantly, Claire climbed onto the picnic table, her gaze fixed on Dave's innocent and silly cute face. She hesitated for a moment, contemplating the leap of faith she was about to take.

"You better catch me," she demanded.

Dave's eyes locked with hers, his determination shined through. "Of course, I will," he insisted, "I'd never let you fall. Trust me."

With a deep breath, Claire propelled herself forward, her body hurtled through the air. Her heart fluttered in her chest as she surrendered herself to Dave's promise. As she fell, her mind briefly lost reality and fear rushed through her veins. But just as she was about to hit the ground, Dave swiftly stepped forward as his reflexes kicked in, and he caught her in his strong arms. The sudden motion caused Dave to lose his balance, and, for a moment, it seemed like they might tumble over.

However, Dave managed to regain his footing, and he pulled Claire back up and safely stabilised them. As they found their balance, Claire found herself looking into Dave's eyes, her heart beating rapidly increased. The intensity in their shared gaze created a moment of undeniable connection, as if time had momentarily frozen around them.

In that instant, the world seemed to fade away, and they were lost in each other's eyes. The chaos of the fall and the subsequent rescue faded into the background as they became completely absorbed in the depth of their emotions. Their silent exchange spoke volumes, conveying something magical. As the moment lingered, they both became aware of the electricity in the air, the unspoken tension that hung between them. Their hearts beat in unison, and a subtle smile tugged at the corners of their lips. It was a defining moment, one that held the promise of something more than mere friendship or chance. The intensity of their connection exploded, leaving both Claire and Dave with a lingering curiosity and the knowledge that something significant had transpired between them.

Claire's cheeks flushed with embarrassment as she instinctively pulled away from Dave's touch. Dave, undeterred by Claire's reaction, gently reached out and took her hand. His touch was warm and reassuring, causing a shiver to run down Claire's spine.

Claire admired Dave's confidence and adventurous spirit, but she couldn't help wondering where their spontaneous escapade would lead them next. "What now, Batman?" she asked hesitantly, with a sound of playfulness and uncertainty.

Dave flashed her a cheeky grin while his eyes gleamed with excitement. With his renewed confidence, he was ready to lead them into the unknown. Dave spotted what looked like an exit door.

"This way," he whispered, his words carried a promise of something extraordinary.

Claire followed closely behind, her nerves pulsating with elation. As she took a step closer, their bodies were now inches apart. Whatever lay ahead, she was ready to face it, hand in hand with her own personal Batman.

CHAPTER 19

~THE BREAK IN~

U nder the cover of darkness, they made their way towards the doors to the building dominating the restricted area. It darkened and emanated an eerie aura. As they approached the entrance, a heavy metal door loomed ominously, tightly fixed on its rusty hinges as if warning away any trespassers. The air surrounding the building was thick with an oppressive silence, broken only by the distant sound of machinery and the steady sound of computers. It was a place shrouded in secrecy and guarded by an unseen force. With determination Dave pressed a button, hoping it would release the lock on the door. A faint click was heard, and to their relief, the door swung open. Without hesitation, Dave gestured for Claire to go ahead and quickly followed her through the door, granting them access to this forbidden place.

Their adventure was not without its challenges. They had to network through dark corridors, avoiding security cameras and guards patrolling the area. Their senses heightened, they relied on each other's quick thinking and agility to stay one step ahead.

Stepping inside, they were engulfed by darkness, except for the occasional flickering fluorescent light overhead. The interior was a quagmire quarry of corridors, each leading to a different purpose, unknown and concealed. The building smelt of dust and decay, mingling with the faint metallic tang of old machinery. The walls, decked with peeling paint, seemed to whisper secrets of the building's forgotten past.

The sound of machines rippled through the halls, an orchestra of mechanical whirs, clanks, and hisses that filled the space. It was a chorus of industry, but unknown to its purpose. The rhythmic pulsation of computers added to the melody, their soft hum permeating the atmosphere like a lullaby sung by unseen entities.

Their adventure was not without its challenges. They had to network through dark corridors, avoiding security cameras and guards patrolling the area. Their senses heightened, they relied on each other's quick thinking and agility to stay one step ahead.

As they ventured deeper into the building, the corridors branched off into various rooms, each with its distinct space. Some were filled with rows of towering servers, their blinking lights casting an otherworldly glow. Others housed laboratories where experiments lay frozen in time, their equipment covered with sheets. The rooms brimmed with forgotten ambitions and unfinished projects, relics of a bygone era.

It was a place where secrets were locked away, hidden from prying eyes. There was a deep sense of foreboding as if the very walls suppressed hidden darkness.

CHAPTER 20

~THE RESTRICTED BUILDING~

The robotic noises resembled those typically heard in machinery industrial sectors. Those familiar noises evoked images of conveyor belts in motion, heavy machinery at work, and the drone of countless moving parts. Whether it was the clattering of metal, the hiss of steam, or the rumble of engines, the automatic sounds transported them into a world of manufacturing and production, where complex systems and intricate mechanisms came together to create products.

As they navigated away from the noises, their ears nervously perked up at the sound of approaching footsteps. The distinct rhythm of heavy feet echoed through the corridors, growing louder with each passing moment. The anticipation built as they wondered who or what was making its way towards them.

Dave's nervousness was tangible as he stood there, uncertainty traced across his face. Clare sensed Dave's uneasiness and instinctively searched for reassurance in his eyes.

Summoning a surge of courage, he mustered his strength and approached the nearest door, his heart raging in his chest. A sudden relief swooped over him when he found it unlocked and without hesitation, he held the door open for Claire, prioritising her safety above his own. With a gentle gesture, he guided her into the room, stepping in afterward, ready to face whatever awaited them.

Their pulses were pounding a forceful rhythm much like the explosive energy of a volcanic eruption. They closed the door behind them and turned to search for a place to hide, but to their dismay, they were faced with a frightening contraption. It looked like a scene from a horror movie. The room was dominated by a dismantled body, tools scattered haphazardly, and various other unsettling objects. It was clear they had stumbled upon something dangerous and scary.

The horrifying object incapacitated them, almost to the point where they nearly forgot about the footsteps.

Dave and Claire stood frozen in shock as they continued to observe the gruesome sight before them. The room was dimly lit, casting eerie shadows on the macabre body suspended mid-air.

Claire's heart raced as she stared at the bizarre scene unfolding before her eyes. She couldn't believe what she was witnessing, and the shock was evident in her voice, "What the fuck?"

The air was engulfed with a grotesque smell. Claire's trembling hands covered her mouth as she tried to suppress a gasp. Her eyes met Dave's, searching for some semblance in his expression. Dave, though visibly disturbed, mustered his courage and took a step forward, fixed on to protect Claire.

With fear and curiosity, they tried to comprehend the nature of this disfigured entity. It possessed a peculiar appearance, appearing to be a distorted amalgamation of human and something else entirely. Suspended in mid-air, it hung by its limbs which were securely fastened to each corner of the room with large, star-shaped metal clamps. The sight was unnerving, as the skin of this abomination dangled from where it had been gruesomely severed, exposing the raw flesh beneath. The scene was made even more disturbing by the absence of its internal organs, which had been mercilessly extracted. The head of this unfortunate being was grotesquely bound, the clamps stretched its skin to the point of near rupture, revealing the cracked and shattered skull beneath.

Once a human body, it now existed in a state of complete and utter dismemberment, a horrifying testament to the unspeakable violence that had been perpetrated upon it.

Finally unable to bear the sight any longer Dave cautiously approached the door, his hands shaking as he reached for the doorknob. With a deep breath, he slowly turned it and pushed the door open, revealing the inescapable symphony of heavy footsteps resonating through the floor. Each step reverberated with undeniable force, growing louder. Claire gripped onto Dave, which she tightened as they braced themselves for whatever was about to happen. They exchanged a quick glance, their eyes filled with terror and panic. He quietly closed the door.

As the group approached them, Claire and Dave pressed themselves against a wall, trying to blend in with the shadows. The body was surrounded by a backdrop of plastic sheets providing some cover, but the pungent metallic smell of blood lingered in the air, making their hiding spot all the more precarious. As they hurried themselves out of sight, Dave accidentally kicked over a bucket of blood. Claire quickly stifled a gasp, her eyes wide with fear as the spilled bucket of blood created a messy pool on the floor. She released her hand and motioned for him to stay quiet, placing a finger over her lips. The footsteps drew nearer, and the tension in the air became unbearable.

Suddenly, the footsteps stopped just outside the room. The silence became suffocating as if the entire world was holding its breath, waiting for the next moment to unfold. Claire and Dave held their breaths, their bodies tense and ready for action. The door opened, and it sounded like a group of people had entered the room. Claire's heart felt like it was about to explode out of her chest. She exchanged a nervous glance with Dave, silently urging him to remain calm. They strained their ears, waiting for any sign that their presence had been detected.

Instantly, a familiar voice was heard. It was Michelle, who appeared to be accompanied by some men. Filled with detachment, she reported that they had removed all of the organs, including the eyeballs, from body 409. Unbeknownst to her and the others, a pool of blood slowly seeped from under the white plastic sheet, unnoticed. One of the men was focused on meeting their deadlines as he inquired about whether all the organs were ready to be shipped on time. Michelle assured him that the organs were currently being transported and that their debts would be covered by tomorrow's transportation.

She indicated that four more bodies were currently in progress, suggesting that their illicit operations were proceeding according to plan. The third man sternly asked to see the paperwork for these actions, seeking validation and assurance that everything was in order. Michelle agreed to show them the paperwork and led them out. As they exited the room, they closed the door behind them. After what felt like an eternity, the footsteps continued past the room, growing fainter with each passing moment.

Though the immediate danger had passed, Claire and Dave stood in shock, surrounded by the pool of blood that bore witness to the unspeakable acts that had taken place. And that they were next. They knew they had to act quickly.

Claire let out a shaky breath. Relieved tears flooded her eyes. She turned to Dave and mouthed a silent, "We're safe for now," before cautiously stepping out from behind the plastic sheets. Claire, desperate to rid themselves of the evidence, stepped cautiously out of the bloody mess, attempting to kick off the stains from her shoes. In her search for something to assist them, she stumbled upon a cloth.

"Try wiping some of the blood off you," Claire insisted with urgency, handing the cloth to Dave. Realising the blood was too much to wipe clean, Claire suggested they remove some of their clothing and shoes. They both understood the importance of leaving no trace behind. Their escape became a race against time, as they strived to put as much distance as possible between themselves and the dangerous secrets they had inadvertently stumbled upon. As they fled the scene, Claire and Dave knew they would have to carry the burden of what they had witnessed. However, they also knew that they had survived, and now their task was to bring the truth to light and ensure that justice prevailed.

Dave and Claire successfully exited the building; they ran towards the fence they originally climbed over, carrying their clothes with fear. The cool breeze brushed against their bare skin, reminding them of their unconventional attire. With each step, they were fuelled by the adrenaline pumping through their veins. Dave, insistent on proving his masculinity, led the way, his trainers and socks clutched tightly in one hand, his jeans in the other. Claire followed closely behind, her leggings draped over her arm, her shoes held roughly in her hand. Their bare feet lightly touched the ground as they crossed the terrain.

As they approached the fence, their hearts raced even faster. They could see their escape route, the familiar panel in the fence that would lead them to freedom. They could almost taste the exhilaration of breaking free from the horrific event, embracing their lives in the open air.

CHAPTER 21

~TWO HEARTS~

D ave and Claire sat in her quiet dimly lit room, their emotions running high after witnessing something so catastrophic that evening. The pressure of their impending decision loomed forcefully over them. Claire expressed her disbelief at the events they had witnessed, and Dave acknowledged the chaotic and disturbing nature of it all. They had both declared their plan to end their unhappy lives the next day, but Dave suggested that perhaps they should reconsider in light of the experiences they've had and shared. Claire was firm that she couldn't continue living in this world, and Dave proposed the idea that things could be different for them.

Claire questioned what Dave meant by 'different'. Dave clarified that he meant them being together. Claire was taken back by the suggestion, prompting Dave to express that he had never met anyone like her before. Claire responded with self-deprecating humour, questioning if she was as messed up as Dave. However, Dave emphasised the connection they shared, believing that they could support and understand each other. Claire expressed her concerns that they could potentially bring each other down, apologising for her negative thinking. In response, Dave appreciated Claire's worries and told her that she was amazing.

Claire prepared another round of drinks, sharing her despair, "I can't keep feeling like I do, I came here to end my pathetic life."

Dave urged Claire to take a chance on their newfound connection, suggesting that they gave it a try. Claire admitted her fear, expressing her apprehension about what lay ahead. Dave, however, felt relieved. He also shared the same fear but emphasised that despite the uncertainty he felt more alive than ever before.

Claire acknowledged the cheesiness of their conversation but admitted the truth behind his words.

Dave took a large sip, gathering his courage, "I've never felt this way about anyone before." Claire felt elated by Dave's revelation, although she needed a moment to process his words. Finally, she responded, "I understand what you're saying, but it doesn't change who we are or how our minds work."

Dave reached out, placing his hand on Claire's arm, "But we just get each other. We know we work as one." Claire, with enthusiasm, contemplated the idea; her mind wrestled with both hope and doubt, "Or we could end upmaking each other worse? I'm sorry for being so pessimistic."

Dave's admiration for Claire shone through his eyes, "You're beautiful inside and out, you know that?"

Claire's face softened, mirroring Dave's sentiment, "And I think you are, too."

Standing up, Dave took a step closer to Claire, his hand still resting on her arm. "Let's give this a shot? Let's try to change our lives, together."

Claire met Dave's gaze, her eyes filled with dreams and worries, "I'm scared."

"Me, too. But for the first time in my life, I feel happy, really happy. I can even feel and hear my heart beating." He pointed to his chest and then gently touched Claire's heart, "And I want yours."

Claire, vulnerable yet hopeful, replied, "As long as

you promise not to break it."

Dave reassured her, declaring that they were united as one and that he would never do anything to harm her.

Tenderly, he stroked the side of her face as they shared a moment of intense connection. Their eyes drew closer, revealing a powerful sexual attraction between them. Without hesitation, their mouths slowly gravitated towards each other, culminating in a passionate and energetic kiss that left them both breathless.

In the heat of the moment, Claire eagerly lifted up Dave's T-shirt, while he swiftly removed her blouse and quickly undid her bra. The intensity of their desire is undeniable, and they couldn't help but express their astonishment at the overwhelming passion they were experiencing. Excitedly, Claire found herself lifted by Dave and gently placed onto her bed. As the anticipation built, he removed her knickers and casually tossed them aside onto the floor.

Claire reciprocated by pulling down Dave's boxer shorts, with his assistance, as they eagerly shed the remnants of clothing that separated them.

Claire was clearly impressed and excited by his manhood, exclaiming, "Wow!"

Dave, eager to please, responded, "I'll give you wow." In a perfect union of bodies and emotions, they engaged in passionate lovemaking, fully immersed in the intimate connection they shared.

He asked, "Do you want me to stop?" "No fucking way!" Dave, seeking clarification, asked if this was her first time. Claire confirmed that it was indeed her first time but urged him not to stop. Their lips met in a passionate kiss, their bodies stuck closer as their arms wrapped around each other. All their worries disappeared, their connection deepened with the exploration of two passionate bodies, and the meaning of their surroundings was drowned out by the intensity of their exciting moment. In this intimate exchange, they communicated their deepest emotions without saying a word. Their eyes spoke volumes, conveying their love, passion, and the unspoken promises they made to each other.

CHAPTER 22

~SEX and DEATH~

Manjit abruptly awakened, startled by the clamorous sounds emanating from the adjacent room, belonging to Claire. The suddenness of the noise disrupted her peaceful slumber, jolting her into a state of wakefulness. As Manjit's consciousness gradually adjusted to the surrounding environment, she found herself exasperated by the cacophony originating from Claire's quarters. Manjit's anger boiled over, her voice fraught with frustration as she gasped, "Is someone taking the piss?" The loud noises that infiltrated her sleep had ignited the fiery edge within her, leaving little room for patience or understanding.

Startled by Manjit's outburst, Sudi placed her book down, her sleep-disoriented mind struggling to grasp the situation. She sat up in her chair, confusion lingered in her voice as she inquired, "What's happened?" Yet, in an instant, realisation dawned upon her, and her tone shifted to one of shock and disbelief. "Oh my word!" Sudi yelled, as the true nature of the sound became clearer to them.

With a sudden burst of energy, Manjit stepped out of her bed, her body jolted into action. However, as she stood up, a sharp pang of pain ran through her body, which caused her to stumble momentarily. The discomfort threatening to overwhelm her, she sat back down on her bed, feeling defeated.

Sudi affectionately told Manjit to stay put, assuring her that she would prepare coffee for both of them. However, the sudden interruption and subsequent commotion had left Manjit feeling bewildered. The perplexing circumstances surrounding the loud noises had left them angry. Meanwhile, Sudi responded to the situation by getting out of her seat and taking charge of brewing the coffee. She nonchalantly remarked, "Sex and death," hinting at the source of the disturbance, indicating a potential connection between passionate encounters and unsettling outcomes.

Manjit, still grappling with the bizarre nature of the situation, expressed her confusion and found it utterly disturbing, "And they're depressed? It's messed up."

Sudi attempted to shift the focus away from the disconcerting happenings and suggested that they forget about them and the noises for the time being. Instead, she proposed enjoying a comforting cup of coffee and engaging in a good old-fashioned chat, seeking time away from the chaos that surrounded them.

CHAPTER 23

~BIG MAN~

Nestled in the cosy confines of their shared bed, Claire and Dave found themselves enveloped in a blissful intimacy. Their laughter reverberated through the room, punctuating the air with the sound of their shared joy. In that tender moment, their bodies entwined and their hearts connected, they revelled in the simple pleasure of each other's company. The world outside may be filled with chaos and uncertainty, but within the sanctuary of their shared space, Claire and Dave created a haven of laughter and affection, finding hope in the warmth of their embrace. The room had been filled with exhaustion and exhilaration.

Breaking the silence, Dave mustered the courage to ask, "Was that okay?"

Claire couldn't help but scoff at his question, pushing

him playfully. "Are you kidding?" she bantered, "As if you didn't know!"

A satisfied grin spread across Dave's face. "Yeah," he admitted, "It was fucking amazing."

Contentment washed over them as Claire placed her head against Dave's chest, relishing in the gentle strokes of his hand through her hair. But within the intimacy, a solemn thought hung in the air.

"We need to let the others know what we saw tonight," Dave finally spoke up, breaking the tranquillity. Claire lifted her head, concern etched on her face.

"They'll think we're even crazier than they already do," she said.

Dave nodded. "Two mentally ill people telling them that their bodies are being used for an organ market?"

"They'd accuse us of having a mental breakdown or think we're just fucked up." A soft giggle escaped Claire's lips. "I mean, would you blame them?" she chuckled. "It does sound far-fetched."

Dave's head slumped slightly, his confidence withering. "I'm not good with words," he confessed, his voice soft with self-doubt. "I doubt they'd believe me even if I tried." Sensing his vulnerability, Claire tried to reassure him. "How about the two of us just leave now?" she suggested, her eyes searching for his agreement.

Dave sat up, contemplating her proposal. "We do need to get out of here," he admitted.

Taking charge, Claire swung her legs over the side of the bed. "Let's pack our stuff now and leave," she declared.

But Dave hesitated, realising the importance of attempting to share their discovery with the others before making their escape. "Can you talk to the others, please?" a glint of desperation in his voice, "We can't leave without at least trying?"

Reluctance crossed Claire's face. "You mean you want me to tell them?" uncertainty laced her words.

Dave nodded; his mind already shifted to practical matters. "I'll make some tea," he offered, hoping to provide a sense of comfort within the impending storm.

Claire hesitated; the pressure of responsibility hung over her. "I'll try."

CHAPTER 24

~ORGANS~

With a nod, Claire left the room, her thoughts whirled around like a vicious storm.

As she made her way to where the others were gathered, she knew that their lives were about to change forever. Claire, wearing one of Dave's long T-shirts and her knickers, quietly knocked on the door of the neighbouring room. As the door swung open, Sudi could sense that something was amiss.

Claire's expression held both worry and urgency, causing a knot to tighten in Sudi's stomach. Sensing Claire's unease, she gently asked, "Can I help you, Claire?"

With an anxious gasp, Claire replied, "I've got something to tell you, well, warn you about."

Sudi invited her in, and Claire entered the room where Manjit was sitting on her bed with a cup of coffee.

Sudi also took a seat, intrigued to hear what important news Claire needed to share.

Manjit asked Claire if her visit was about the noise coming from her room. Confused, Claire asked her what noise they were referring to. Manjit and Sudi exchanged looks of disbelief.

Manjit, annoyed by the late-night interruption, "Never mind. What can we do for you at this time of night?"

Undeterred, Claire took a deep breath and began to explain, "This is going to sound crazy, but it's important. I couldn't sleep, neither could Dave, so we decided to have a look next door in the restricted area."

Manjit interrupted, her frustration evident, "But we can't access that area. We're not allowed. How did you get in?"

With her hands rubbing nervously together, Claire informed them both that they managed to sneak in through a back door, out at the back. Sudi, who felt worn out, asked "So what do you want to tell us?"

Claire hesitated for a moment, then blurted out that they saw something disturbing and that the clinic was using human bodies to sell their organs.

Manjit and Sudi looked straight at each other and let out a loud chuckle.

"What kind of rubbish do we have to listen to now," Manjit asked, shaking her head and exhaling an irritated sigh. Claire's emotions were evident as she confronted Manjit, questioning her sense of entitlement. Her response was curt and unsympathetic, further exacerbating Claire's frustration and pain. Feeling misunderstood, she turned to leave, expressing her exasperation at this lack of comprehension regarding mental illness. Sudi, who had been silently observing, offered a soothing suggestion for Claire to rest and gain clarity in the morning. Overwhelmed with disappointment, Claire's eyes filled with tears as she expressed regret for trying to warn them. Seeking solace, she retreated to her room where Kay, noticing her distress, reached out with concern. Claire, visibly troubled, confided in Kay, accepting the invitation for a heart-to-heart conversation in search of comfort and empathy.

Meanwhile Manjit and Sudi engaged in a conversation within the confines of Manjit's room. Sudi voiced her uncertainties, questioning the veracity of

Claire's claims. Manjit, finding amusement in the situation, dismissed the notion of truth, citing Claire's recent intimate encounter as evidence of her unreliability. Despite Manjit's scepticism, Sudi persisted in her contemplation, finding Claire's revelations peculiar and warranting further consideration. Expressing her lingering doubts, Sudi pondered the possibility of hidden motives behind Claire's warning, drawing attention to a nearby restricted building that triggered her curiosity. Manjit, disinterested in entertaining Sudi's suspicions, chose to disregard her inquiries, opting to focus on enjoying their remaining time together free from troubling thoughts. Frustrated by Manjit's dismissiveness, Sudi proposed a daring question regarding the mysterious activities within the restricted building, hinting at a darker undercurrent that lingered beneath the surface of their tranquil environment.

Sudi expressed her doubts, asking, "What if she's telling the truth?"

Manjit, bemused at the idea, "Truth? She was just having sex with that bloke a few minutes ago."

Sudi persisted, "It just seems really strange that she would tell us something like that." "Probably just some sick mind game she's playing."

Sudi wasn't ready to let go of her suspicions. She then suggested, "Maybe we should ask what that building is for? And ask them what they do with all the bodies?"

Manjit, now extremely irritated, "Yeah, why don't we ask them for a tour too!"

Sudi pleaded, "Don't get wound up, sweetheart. I just think we should be careful."

Manjit straightened her bed covers her as she laid back into bed. She refused to take it seriously and couldn't resist one last snap, "We could even ask them to put all the dead bodies on display."

The harsh lights in Marcus and Kay's room flickered, casting an eerie glow on the pale walls. Kay looked at Marcus, her eyes gleamed with determination and love, "I'm going to take you home where you belong." There was a brief pause, then she continued, "We need you Marcus, more than you could possibly imagine. You're still you, the man I love and adore."

Marcus, feeling torn and unsure, hesitated to respond. He understood the gravity of the situation and the importance of why they were there. Yet, there was a part of him that longed for the comfort and familiarity of home. Before he could articulate his thoughts, Kay stood up and walked towards him. With tenderness in her touch, she placed her hands on his face, her eyes searching his for a sign of agreement.

"What they're doing here is immoral," Kay asserted, "I'm begging you, let's go home. I married you through better or worse, sickness and health. I'll be damned to let them take you." As Kay spoke those heartfelt words, a single tear escaped from Marcus's eye, rolling down his cheek like a silent testament to their love and the immense struggle they faced together. In that tear, there was a mixture of fear, hope, and a burning desire to reclaim control of their lives.

And so, in that room, surrounded by uncertainty and death, Kay and Marcus made their decision. They chose to defy the odds, to embrace the unknown, and to fight for their love against all odds.

CHAPTER 25

~CAUGHT IN THE ACT~

An hour later, Dave and Claire, still groggy from sleep, frantically scrambled to cover themselves up as Michelle and the two armed security men entered the room. The sudden intrusion startled them, and they exchanged baffled glances. Michelle greeted them both with a cheerful but scornful "Good morning." Claire, clearly alarmed by Michelle's sudden appearance, expressed her disapproval at their unannounced entry. Michelle, however, disagreed with Claire's objection, citing her concern and the fact that she had knocked before entering.

Dave, who had remained silent up to this point, suddenly demanded to know the reason for their presence. Michelle's gaze shifted between Claire and Dave as she insisted on receiving an explanation for last night's trespassing. Tensions filled the room as the group stood facing each other, each waiting for the other to provide clarification on the unexpected visit.

Claire, attempting to quell her rising anger, expressed their desire to avoid any conflicts and apologised if they had unknowingly violated any rules. Michelle's demeanour softened as she assured them that whatever they thought they had witnessed the previous night was unrelated to the activities taking place in the building.

Despite Michelle's reassurances, Claire's suspicion lingered, suggesting a dark motive behind the mysterious events. Dismissing the notion of organ trafficking, Michelle clarified that the bodies they had seen were donated for scientific research purposes. When Dave inquired about the nature of the research, Michelle explained that their team of medical researchers dedicated their efforts to discovering treatments for human ailments.

Claire remained suspicious, voicing her disbelief in the face of Michelle's explanations. Convinced of their own observations, she emphasised their awareness and intelligence, rejecting Michelle's account. Growing frustrated by Claire's persistent doubts, Michelle turned to Dave, appealing to his naivety and asking him to intervene in the conversation. Michelle believed that Dave, a follower, could understand their story behind their activities and help dispel Claire's suspicions.

Dave, feeling the urgency to resolve the escalating situation, attempted to propose a solution and mend the damage. His desperation was visible as he sought a way to rectify the unfolding crisis. Claire, recognising the severity of the circumstances and the jeopardy they were in, decided to play along with the facade, acknowledging the gravity of the situation they found themselves in.

Michelle, unaffected by their pleas and attempts at reconciliation, maintained her stoic demeanour. She dismissed their efforts, emphasising the futility of trying to rectify the situation at that late stage. With a slow shake of her head, Michelle conveyed a sense of finality, indicating that it was too late for any form of reconciliation or redemption.

Following her decisive statement, Michelle and the security guards exited the room, leaving Dave and Claire behind to grapple with the consequences of their actions. As the door closed shut behind them, a heavy silence descended upon the room, amplifying the weight of the situation and the irreversible nature of their choices. The reality of their predicament sank in, leaving Dave and Claire overwhelmed with a sense of confusion and deep regret, realising that there was no turning back from the repercussions of their actions.

As Kay and Marcus exited their room, eager to leave, a voice called out to them. It was Michelle, the strict and no-nonsense lady. With a concerned expression on her face, she approached the pair, determined to understand their intentions. "Hello! And where might you two be going?"

Kay, ever the calming one, responded with a polite smile, "Hi, Michelle! We're leaving. Change of heart, you know how it is?"

A heavy sigh escaped Michelle's lips, betraying her apprehension. She had feared this response. Turning her attention towards the second security guard nearby, she issued a firm command, "Escort them back to their room immediately. Do not let anyone leave. Understood? No one leaves today!"

Without further ado, Michelle walked away. Meanwhile, Kay stood in place with Marcus by her side, bewildered by the sudden turn of events. Kay wore a look of disbelief as she turned to the guard.

"What? I don't understand. What's going on? Why can't we leave?" she asked.

The security guard, a towering figure with an air of authority, fixed his gaze upon them. His voice resonated with forcefulness as he delivered his instructions, "Get back into your room. It's for your safety and the safety of others."

Though confused and disheartened, Kay and Marcus reluctantly complied with the guard's orders. However, they weren't sure what to do next. They slowly turned around, their dreams of venturing back home temporarily dashed. With heavy hearts, they went back towards their room.

Manjit found herself caught in the middle of a mysterious and tense situation. Confused and worried, she stepped out of her room and found herself face-to-face with two security guards.

"What is going on?" she demanded.

The two security guards exchanged a quick glance before Security 2 sternly replied, "Stay in your rooms. Now." Manjit's exploded, "Why? What's happening?"

Security 1, with his commanding and angry tone

responded, "Just get back to your room and close the door."

Manjit was furious, wanting answers so she could understand the confusing situation unfolding around her. She defiantly stood her ground, "I won't comply until you tell me why? I'm standing here until I know what the hell is going on!"

However, Security 1's patience wore thin, and he reached for his pistol, a clear display of authority with dire consequences. "Do as you're told," Security 1 warned her, full of threat, "I don't want to have to hurt anyone, but you're not helping yourself."

The tension in the air grew almost visible as Manjit weighed her options. Just as she contemplated her next move, a familiar voice interrupted from behind her.

"Just close the door, Manjit!" Sudi forcefully instructed her, as she tried pulling Manjit back into the room. She could see there was an immediate danger.

Understanding the intensity of the situation, Sudi's words carried a wisdom that resonated with Manjit. Realising that her safety and the safety of others was at stake, Manjit reluctantly listened to Sudi's advice. She hesitated for a moment, her eyes met with Sudi's, before she finally nodded in agreement. With a bewildered heart and a mind filled with unanswered questions, Manjit retreated to her room, closing the door behind her. As the latch clicked shut, Manjit couldn't help but wonder about the events evolving just beyond the confines of their room. The mysteries of this set up now consumed her thoughts, and she was focused on uncovering the truth once the chaos subsided.

Meanwhile, in Claire's room, she attempted to widen the small open window at the top of a main window, but despite her efforts, she discovered that they did not open. It seemed that they may be either stuck or designed to remain closed. Dave proceeded to put on his clothes. "We've gotta find a way out of here!" Claire called out, as she stepped down from the desk, then looked around with urgency - glaring back at the window.

Dave, feeling the pressure, asked Claire, "How? What can we do?"

Claire, unable to contain her frustration, snapped back, "Well, I thought you were the mastermind? Seeing as it's your fault we're in this mess." Confusion exploded from Dave's face as he asked, "What do you mean? How is it my fault?"

Realising that blaming each other wouldn't solve anything, Claire let out a sigh of defeat, "Just forget what I said, I'm just upset," she proclaimed, abandoning her attempt to escape through the window. Dave understood her feelings and didn't let her words of blame affect him. Instead he thought about what he could do to help the situation. He wanted to make Claire feel safe in his company.

CHAPTER 26

~THE ESCAPE~

Dave felt remorseful, and he approached Claire and embraced her tightly. "I'm sorry," he whispered sincerely.

Claire, her anger and frustration subsiding, responded, "Me, too. It's not your fault. That woman is a psycho."

Seeking ideas to abandon this crisis, Dave walked towards the door, contemplating a way to outsmart their captors. "If I can break the swipe recognition on the door," he mused, "maybe it could prevent them from coming in."

Claire, concerned about being trapped even if they managed to disable the door's security, voiced her uncertainty, "But we'd still be stuck in here."

As they stood in that trapped room, their minds raced with ideas, searching for a solution that would ensure both their escape and their freedom.

Dave was in a desperate situation, searching for something sharp to aid their escape. He quickly spotted a pen and a hair clip on the desk and grabbed them. Determined to find a way, he considered smashing the window as a possible way out. With a sense of urgency, Dave tampered with the swipe door key box, managing to detach it from the wall. Turning to Claire, he requested her fob key card, hoping it would grant them access. Claire handed it over, and Dave proceeded to swipe the card, but to their disappointment, the door remained locked.

Undeterred, Dave commented that their action should at least keep unwanted individuals out. In a bold move, he grabbed a half-full bottle of vodka and hurled it at the window, causing it to crack. Seizing a chair, Dave forcefully threw it at the broken window, shattering the remaining glass. Amidst the chaos, Claire was in shock.

Dave, discovering their way out was now clear, assisted Claire through the window before jumping out, ensuring their escape. Together they knew they could conquer anything.

As the security guards desperately attempted to open

the door, their frustration grew. One of them, outraged with anger and determination, delivered a powerful kick that splintered the door. With a loud bang, the door swung open, and the guard rushed towards the window. As he reached it, he caught a glimpse of Dave and Claire fleeing into the distance. The guard spat on the ground to help calm his distress. He cursed them under his breath, knowing that his pursuit would be in vain.

The guard quickly assessed the situation fully, attaining that there was no point in chasing after Dave and Claire on foot. He radioed for backup, where he provided a description of the escaping individuals, hoping that his fellow security personnel would intercept them. The guard's focus now shifted to reporting the incident to his superiors and ensuring that the premises were secure. He knew that an investigation would be launched to determine how Dave and Claire managed to infiltrate the building and escape.

Sudi and Manjit found themselves in turmoil after hearing the dramatic banging and smashing. As they caught their breath, Manjit couldn't help but voice her frustration. "What the hell is going on in this bloody place?" she blurted, verbalising her anger whilst on the verge of tears.

Sudi, trying to keep a level head, suggested calling the police.

Realising that they couldn't continue being locked up like prisoners in this hellish nightmare, Manjit reached for her mobile phone, determined to make the call. However, she suddenly realised that she didn't know the number for the local police. Turning to Sudi, she wondered, "What's the number to ring them, Mum?"

Sudi admitted, "Oh, I don't know."

Teary eyed, they needed to find the number quickly, Manjit started searching on her mobile phone. After a few moments, she announced: "Here it is!" With the number in hand, Manjit dialled the police.

The voice on the other end of the line answered, "Halla, polis?"

Manjit, relieved to have reached someone, pleaded, "Hello, please can you help us? We're held prisoners at the Swedish Euthanasia Clinic."

The police officer responded in Swedish, "Du ar engelsk?"

Confused and exasperated, Manjit professed, "Sorry, I don't understand. I don't speak Swedish. Do you speak

English?"

The officer attempted to communicate again, asking, "Vad ar problemet?" (What is the problem?)

Disappointing as this was, she knew the language barrier was hindering their communication, Manjit became even more aggravated, "Could you find someone who speaks English, please?" she begged.

Unfortunately, the officer on the other end of the line couldn't understand Manjit's request and continued speaking in Swedish. Feeling dejected and disgruntled, Manjit hung up her phone. "I don't know how much more I can take!" she shouted, with extreme disappointment of failure. Sudi, tried to provide some comfort, by reducing the seriousness, "Take it they don't speak English?"

Manjit, cramped by the circumstances, surmised her thoughts, "I'm going to end up killing myself at this rate," she inferred, feeling like the whole world was against her. Sudi and Manjit were left feeling trapped and desperate, unsure of what their next move would be. Sudi, tried to offer some perspective, "Maybe god is telling us something?"

But Manjit couldn't see past her pain, "Or maybe he

wants to punish me and have the last laugh before I die."

Sudi made a heartfelt plea, "Let's go home, Manjit." she said gently, understanding that Manjit needed love and support more than anything else. "I need you. I will care for you and do whatever is needed to make your final months comfortable."

Manjit, overwhelmed by Sudi's offer, hesitated, "I can't ask you to do that, Mum. Anyway, I might only have weeks. I don't want to put you through it all. It would be too much."

"I would give up my life just to have an extra day with you," Sudi declared, her eyes glazed with emotion, "I would sacrifice my soul to be with you until the end."

"I don't know what to do now, Mum," she confessed, finally opening up about her inner turmoil.

Sudi embraced her tightly. "Oh, sweetheart, I've been waiting for you to open up," she whispered softly, "Please let me take you home where you belong."

Manjit, touched by Sudi's pure love and support, asked, "Are you sure, Mum?"

Sudi looked into Manjit's eyes, and her conviction shined through. "If only you knew how sure I am."

Feeling a glow of hope, Manjit gathered her strength,

"Well, these idiots need to let us out." Rushing towards the door, she banged on it and shouted, "Let us out now!"

Together Manjit and Sudi were ready to face the challenges that were inevitable, adamant to cling onto the remaining time they had together.

CHAPTER 27

~RUNAWAY~

Claire and Dave sprinted towards the tall exit gates. The gates were surrounded by 6-foot fencing, creating an imposing barrier. However, the severity of their situation pushed them to overcome this obstacle. Dave, exhausted and out of breath, struggled to keep up with Claire's pace. He could feel his muscles burning and his lungs gasping for air. Each step seemed heavier than the last, but he knew he couldn't afford to slow down.

As they frantically made their way towards the exit, the sounds of relentless guards grew louder. The guards were accompanied by barking dogs, adding an extra layer of pressure to their escape. The adrenaline coursing through their veins urged them to run faster, desperate to put distance between themselves and their pursuers.

With the exit gate a mere 100 yards away, Claire

could almost taste freedom. However, her heart sank as she glanced back and noticed Dave stumble and fall to the ground.

She rushed to his rescue, helped him up, and supported his weight, knowing that they needed to keep moving. The guards and dogs were getting closer, and they couldn't afford to waste any more time. Claire tried her hardest to help him, but it severely slowed them down.

Dave yelled, "Get out of here Claire! Run and get help. Please, baby, run!"

She knew she had to make a difficult decision: continue running towards the gate or risk getting caught by the guards.

Dave shouted out one last time, trying to catch his breath, "Meet me at the airport, we're going home together."

Claire continued to run, feeling her heart punching in her chest, fuelled by fear. Her mind raced with thoughts of what might happen to Dave if he got caught. She tried to block out the images of Dave being captured, hoping that he would find a way to escape.

As Claire reached the fence, she felt a surge of

adrenaline and sprinted even faster. With determination in her eyes, she propelled herself toward the 6-foot fence, preparing to grip it tightly and climb over.

As she approached the fence, Claire extended her arms, reaching for the top. She jumped, using her momentum to launch herself upward. Her fingers found purchase on the edge of the fence, and she tightened her grip, her muscles straining with the effort. With a swift, powerful motion, Claire hoisted herself up, her legs kicking to gain leverage. She used her upper body strength to pull her torso over the fence, feeling the rough surface scrape against her skin.

The adrenaline coursing through her veins pushed her onward, and she mustered every ounce of energy to complete the climb. As her legs dangled on the other side of the fence, Claire swung over, her heart was flapping in her chest. With one final push, she propelled herself off the fence, landing on the other side with a resounding thud. She quickly regained her balance and took a moment to catch her breath and steady herself.

Looking back at the fence she just scaled, Claire felt a sense of accomplishment and relief. She knew she had overcome an obstacle, both physically and mentally.

Claire's surroundings blurred as she ran through unfamiliar territory. She dodged obstacles in her path, her instincts guided her through the maze-like streets. She took quick glances behind her, as she searched for any sign of pursuit, but she saw nothing except the empty streets stretching out into the distance. With each passing moment, Claire's fear began to subside, replaced by a growing sense of hope. She started to believe that she might actually make it out of this nightmare. She pushed herself to go even faster, her breath was coming in short, ragged gasps.

After what felt like an eternity, Claire spotted a dimly lit alleyway up ahead. Without hesitation, she veered into it, hoping it would provide her with some much-needed cover. She slowed down her pace, which allowed a moment to catch her breath and assess her surroundings. As the adrenaline began to fade, Claire's body trembled with exhaustion and fear. She took another moment to steady herself, her mind racing with thoughts of what to do next. She knew she couldn't stay in one place for long, but she also needed to find a safe haven—a place where she could regroup and figure out her next move.

With renewed self-belief, Claire pushed herself

forward once again. She understood the road ahead wouldn't be easy, but she was fixed on fighting for her man. She took a few deep breaths, squared her shoulders, and continued on, ready to seek help so she could save Dave and the others. As she continued running, Claire's senses remained heightened. Every sound, every movement felt magnified as she navigated through the unknown terrain. With each step, she pushed away the fear and focused on finding a way to escape any further danger.

CHAPTER 28

~THE SEARCH~

Dave stumbled into the airport in Sweden, his body battered and worn. He was wearing blood-stained jeans and trainers, evidence of the ordeal he had endured. His dishevelled appearance drew the attention of those around him. He stood frozen for a moment, his gaze vacant as blood trickled down from a cut above his right eye. His hair was a mess, adding to the disarray of his overall appearance.

A sudden wave of panic washed over Dave, as he scanned the area, searching for his beloved Claire. His eyes fell upon a series of TV screens displaying airport information, but the overwhelming chaos made it difficult for him to focus. Determined to find help, he limped about with a troubled expression, finally discovering a help service counter. He unintentionally knocked over a sign on the desk, causing a clatter that attracted the attention of the Helpdesk man.

Helpdesk Man addressed Dave in a distinct Swedish accent, "You look like you've had one hell of a day."

"Yeah, you could say that."

Curiously, Helpdesk Man tried to ease the tension. "How can I help you, Sir?"

Dave took a short breath before responding. "I'm looking for a woman."

Helpdesk Man couldn't help but crack a joke, "Have you tried a dating site, sir?"

Dave's ground out, "That might be funny if it wasn't today. Her name is Claire."

Helpdesk Man realised Dave was being serious, so he further inquired, "Claire who?"

Dave's frustration subsided as he admitted, "I don't know her surname."

Helpdesk Man paused for a moment, "Right..."

Feeling defeated, Dave waved his hand, "Forget it."

As Dave turned to leave, Helpdesk Man muttered under his breath, "Will be happy too."

Dave walked urgently towards the sign for the toilets, noticing that the sign was pointing towards a corridor on the right. He quickened his pace, feeling a sense of relief.

As he approached the corridor, he spotted a door at the end with a sign that displayed 'Restrooms' in bold letters. Dave pushed open the door and entered small, well-maintained restroom. The room was well-lit, with a row of sinks on one side and a row of cubicles on the other. He quickly located an unoccupied cubicle and rushed inside, grateful for the privacy.

Dave let out a deep breath, relieved that he made it in time. He couldn't wait a moment longer before attending to his urgent needs. After he finished up, he washed his hands thoroughly at one of the sinks. Dave stepped out of the airport toilets, frustration engraved on his face. He checked the departure screens once again, desperately searching for the next available flights to London. The earliest one was in two hours, and the wait to see if Claire would turn up seemed interminable.

Dave glanced around several times. He noticed that the check-in desk for the next London-bound flight hadn't even opened yet. He sighed heavily, feeling a pang of annoyance at the lack of urgency displayed by the airport staff. Determined to be close to the desk when it finally opened, he found a seat strategically positioned for optimal visibility.

Time seemed to crawl as Dave sat there, his eyelids heavy with fatigue. He fought to stay awake, his mind a whirlwind of impatience and fear. Uncertainty began to wane, and he wondered if he would ever see Claire again. Just as his exhaustion threatened to overpower him, a sudden commotion caught his attention. A couple nearby was engaged in a heated argument about money. It was a spectacle that drew the attention of onlookers, including Dave. He couldn't help but be momentarily distracted as he watched the unfolding drama.

Lost in the chaos of the couple's dispute, Dave missed the entrance of Claire who was frantically searching for him. Her eyes darted through the crowds, a sense of worry and desperation overtaking her. She weaved through the bustling crowd, her mind flooded with emotions. She scanned every seat, hoping for a glimpse of Dave's familiar face, but he was nowhere to be seen. As time passed, Claire's anxiety deepened. She started asking nearby people if they had seen Dave, describing him and providing any distinguishing details she could think of. Some people shook their heads, caught off guard by her distress, while others tried to help by suggesting places he might have gone. Claire's mind was blocked, she considered various possibilities. Did he get lost? Did something happen to him? She tried to push away the worst-case scenarios, but her imagination started to run wild. She retraced her steps, thinking back to their last conversation and the plans they had made. She wondered if there were any hints or clues she might have missed. With each passing minute, Claire's desperation grew.

As the search continued, Claire's emotions fluctuated between fear and frustration. She had already informed the authorities, reporting Dave as missing and providing them with all the necessary details.

Feeling a mixture of bewilderment and frustration, Dave rubbed his temples, questioning the choices that had led him to this point. He needed a moment to gather his thoughts and regain composure. Stepping outside, he spotted a stranger smoking nearby and mustered the courage to approach him. "Excuse me," Dave said in a friendly manner. "Don't suppose you can spare a cigarette, mate?"

The stranger, sensing Dave's distress, responded with a sympathetic smile. Without hesitation, he handed him a cigarette and offered him a light. As the smoke from the cigarette swirled around him, Dave took a deep drag, hoping that the temporary relief would help clear his mind. As Dave took another long drag from the cigarette, he tried to calm his racing thoughts. The smoke filled his lungs, momentarily providing a sense of relief. He looked around, taking in the surroundings outside the airport terminal. The stranger who gave him the cigarette leant against the wall, puffing on his own smoke.

Dave, full of exasperation, angrily threw his cigarette butt onto the ground. He decided to go back inside the airport and find a place to sit. Scanning the area, he spotted some empty seats tucked away at the side. He walked swiftly towards them, not paying attention to his surroundings. In his haste, he accidentally bumped into someone, causing the person to make a disapproving tut. Realising his mistake, Dave quickly apologised to the person he collided with. However, his attention was quickly diverted as he noticed someone standing close to the person he bumped into. At first glance, he hoped it might be Claire.

Apprehensively, he took a closer look. His heart started racing as he confirmed that it was indeed Claire, the love of his life, standing before him. Overwhelmed with shock and love, Dave's emotions intensified. He could hardly believe that Claire was here at the airport with him. The sight of her filled his heart with incredible excitement and happiness. Dave's voice ignited with eagerness as he passionately called out. Growing even louder, his voice caught her attention.

Claire swiftly rotated round. When she locked eyes with Dave, her face instantly illuminated with joy. Relief flooded over her, tears streamed down her face, and she sprinted towards him, embracing him tightly, grateful beyond words that he was safe.

"I've been looking everywhere for you, Dave." Claire sobbed.

"I managed to get away," Dave said, exhausted and happy. "I walked all the way here, hoping to find you."

Their reunion was filled with overwhelming emotions. Claire couldn't believe her luck. She had felt sick with worry ever since she left Dave's side, but now, in this moment, everything felt right again.

Unable to contain her happiness, Claire leaned in and kissed Dave passionately. It was a moment of pure bliss, as if all the troubles and hardships they had faced vanished in that single instant. As they pulled away from the kiss, Dave's concern shifted to their friends, Manjit and Kay. He asked Claire about their whereabouts, hoping they had managed to escape the same fate he had.

"They should be here, somewhere." Claire explained, "The police rescued them after you escaped."

"Yes! That's what I needed to hear!" Dave exclaimed with triumph. "It's incredible! You, me, here and the others are free."

Claire nodded. "Yes, the police came and arrested everyone there. They took our statements and then brought us here." A wide smile spread over her face.

Dave's heart swelled with pride for them all, especially Claire. Although they had faced a great ordeal, they had managed to escape and find safety. And now, with Claire by his side, he felt a renewed sense of happiness and strength.

"I feel so bloody happy now that you're here," Claire said, her eyes sparkled with love and gratitude.

Dave smiled and pulled her closer. "That's my beautiful girl," he whispered. Dave smiled and laughed as he noticed Marcus approaching. He cheerfully bent to Marcus's level, delighted to see him. Dave picked up Marcus's hand and they exchanged a high-five. Dave snorted more laughter, and they both cheered a howling sound. Kay laughed as she observed their interaction then hugged Dave. She then stroked Claire's arm, a sign of gratitude for alerting the police.

Meanwhile, Manjit and Sudi approached the group, waving their hands in a friendly exaggerated manner. Claire and the others joined in the laughter, sharing a special bond formed from a surreal and emotional day. What started as a sad and bewildering situation, ironically ended in a moment filled with camaraderie and happiness.

"I'm sorry for being such a bitch," Manjit confessed to Claire with sincerity. "I was just scared. I shouldn't have judged you."

Claire understood the vulnerability in Manjit's words, so she extended her hand. "Friends?" she asked.

Manjit hesitated for a moment, then took Claire's hand firmly. "Friends," she gratefully accepted.

Manjit, eager to move forward, addressed the group. "Has everyone got their boarding passes?" she asked, hoping that the logistics were in order.

Dave, uncertain what to do, spoke up, "I haven't got any money or anything."

Claire remembered her encounter at the check-in desk and chimed in with a solution. "The lady at the desk said there were spare seats," she explained. "I'll call my mum and ask her to sort it out. She sorted mine out."

Dave's face lifted with gratitude. "Would she do that for me?" he asked.

Claire reassured him, a smile resting on her lips, "Yeah. Surprisingly, she seemed happy to help out." She scanned the area for a payphone. Spotting one nearby, she made her way towards it.

"Tell her I'll pay it all back." Claire, with a mischievous sparkle in her eyes, teasingly responded, "I can think of another way you could pay me back?"

Dave's face lit up with a cheeky grin. "Come here you!" he demanded, as he pulled Claire into a tight embrace.

Overwhelmed with joy, Claire wrapped her arms around Dave, revelling in the newfound future before them. "It's you and me now," she whispered.

Dave announced, "I love you, Claire. I really love you."

Claire's eyes shone with happiness. She couldn't help but reciprocate the sentiment, "And I really love you,

Mister."

As they kissed with intensity, onlookers were captivated by the couple's passion, and some of them even stopped to watch and smile with joy. Kay and Manjit responded by clapping, while Sudi and Marcus were moved to tears.

And so, amidst the busy airport terminal, a group of once-strangers found themselves united, not only by their unexpected journey but also by a newfound bond of friendship and love. With their boarding passes secured and their hearts filled with hope, they embarked on their next adventure, ready to face whatever challenges lay ahead, good or bad, knowing that whatever happened, they would conquer it. Dave lifted Claire off the ground and spun her around. The couple then paused looking into each other's eyes as their souls became one. Feeling the inner force between them, they knew then that this was what was meant to happen. Everyone around them enjoyed the beautiful moment they shared. Dave and Claire's connection was undeniable, as if they had been destined to meet.

From that moment on, Dave and Claire embraced their shared madness, their journey becoming a tapestry of extraordinary experiences. They danced under moonlit nights, climbed mountains at dawn, and laughed until their cheeks ached. Their love was a constant reminder that life was indeed a dream, a beautiful and unpredictable one at that.

As the years passed, Dave and Claire's love story became legendary in the little town where they settled together. People admired their fearlessness and their ability to find joy in the simplest of moments. They inspired others to let go of their inhibitions and embrace the magic that life had to offer. And so Dave and Claire's mad dream continued, their love story forever imprinted in the hearts of those who witnessed it. For they had discovered that sometimes, the most extraordinary adventures begin with two crazy people falling in love.

CHAPTER 29

~A FUTURE TIMELINE~

MANJIT

Manjit travelled back home with her mum. They gathered at a family meeting to discuss the care of Manjit when she fell seriously ill. They all worked together, planning care and support between them. Manjit decided to conceal her relationship with a woman from her family, to avoid further suffering. Manjit made the difficult decision to end her relationship with Sarah, acknowledging that she had to prioritise her family over their love.

This choice left both of them devastated, their hearts shattered. However, Manjit found that deceiving Sarah was even more agonising than facing the prospect of her own death. She deeply cared for Sarah and believed that Sarah shouldn't witness her decline and suffer alongside her.

To ensure that Sarah understood the truth, Manjit took the time to write her a lengthy letter. She couldn't leave this world without Sarah knowing the truth. In this letter, Manjit revealed the real reason behind their separation and expressed the depth of her love for Sarah. She confessed that if circumstances had been different, she would have wanted to spend the rest of her life with her beloved partner. Respecting the importance of this letter, Sudi promised Manjit that she would deliver the letter to Sarah after Manjit's passing.

Manjit lived an extra 8 months, experiencing a range of emotions and moments throughout that time. On days when she felt more mobile, she dedicated herself to enjoying precious family time and exploring the beautiful locations in the UK.

However, there were also days when she had to stay in bed, trying to manage her pain. Despite the challenges, being in the presence of her family brought immense joy to Manjit, and she deeply appreciated their incredible support and kindness. As Manjit entered her last month of life, her health started to deteriorate significantly. It was a painful sight for her family to witness, but they remained grateful for the time they had shared with her.

Eventually, Manjit received palliative care and her morphine dosage was increased to provide comfort. Surrounded by her loved ones, Manjit peacefully passed away. Before her departure, Manjit had left a heartfelt letter to her parents. Overwhelmed by grief, it took them several months to gather the courage to read it, as they tried to navigate through the depths of their loss.

MANJIT POJAB RIP

Dead Mum and Dad,

First and foremost, I want to express my heartfelt gratitude for the immense love, care, and kindness you have shown me throughout my entire life. From the day I entered this world, you have been there for me, and I am truly thankful that you brought me into this beautiful existence. You have been my guiding light, teaching me valuable lessons on strength, courage, and love. I cherished every single moment of my life, and I am grateful for the experiences and opportunities I have had.

I understand that my absence will bring you sadness, and it pains me to think of the grief you will endure.

However, I ask one thing of you, my dear mother and father. Please do not let your sorrow consume you. Allow yourself to feel the pain, to grieve, and then find the strength to embrace life once again. Make the most of the time you have left with as much happiness as you can muster. Do it not only for yourselves but also for me. Although I may no longer be physically present, I know that I will be watching over you, checking in on you from wherever I may be. If you ever feel a pang of pain, it is my way of nudging you to seize the best that life has to offer while you still can. Please always remember that my love for you is eternal, and I will forever be by your side, even in spirit. I want to thank you for all the love, care, and kindness you have given me since the day I was born. I'm thankful you gave birth to me as I had the opportunity to live a wonderful life. You taught me how to be strong, fearless, and loving. I don't regret a single moment of my life.

Live out the time you have left with as much happiness as you can. Do it for me, my beautiful mum and dad. And remember I'll be watching and checking on you.

I will always love you. And I'll always be by your side.

Don't ever forget that.

Love you forever and forever. Manjit xxxxxxxx

CHAPTER 30

~NEW BEGINNINGS~

MARCUS and KAY

After ongoing therapy and receiving a great deal of support, Marcus was able to adapt to his new lifestyle. He made a conscious effort to reset his mind and accept his new self, working hard to manage his thoughts and emotions during moments of hopelessness. A significant source of strength for Marcus was his family. Seeing Kay's face every day and witnessing his son's growth brought him immense joy and gratitude. He realised that his presence, despite the challenges he faced, was a source of comfort for his family, sparing them the pain and heartbreak of his absence. Marcus's family constantly reminded him of their deep appreciation for his contagious smile each day. His son, Arlo, took delight in sharing his aspirations and plans for the future with his father. Arlo's academic excellence and eagerness to impart knowledge to his dad filled Marcus with immense pride.

Meanwhile, Kay continued to work as an accounts secretary, finding fulfilment in her job. She cherished the moments when she could come home and cook for her family, relishing the opportunity to spend quality time with them. As time passed, Marcus grew accustomed to his new routine. He spent his days engrossed in watching football matches, enjoying his favourite television series, and basking in the beauty of the rising and setting sun. He also took the initiative to learn how to use computerised communication programs and systems, acquiring new IT skills along the way.

Additionally, he discovered the world of coding and developed a learning application specifically designed for individuals in situations similar to his own.

CHAPTER 31

~ONE TRUE LOVE~

DAVE and CLAIRE

Dave and Claire's love for one other was truly remarkable. Their bond had grown so profoundly that it surpassed any love ever witnessed. It may sound sickening to some, but their connection was awe-inspiring. It seemed as though their souls were intertwined, making them inseparable. They complemented each other perfectly and existed as a unified entity. Together, they formed a flawless couple who continuously supported and encouraged one another to become the best versions of themselves. Of course, they were not completely without their flaws, but in terms of love between two individuals, they embodied what had to be close to perfection.

Dave and Claire had their fair share of low days.

Occasionally, their minds generated negative thoughts that led to an unhappy state. However, what set them apart was their ability to work through these moments together. They tackled these challenges by either finding humour in the situation or by giving each other the necessary space, time, and support to process their emotions. They possessed a deep understanding of one another and actively assisted in managing each other's emotional well-being.

On the other hand, their good days outnumbered the bad ones. During these positive times, they embarked on long walks, explored various routes, and embraced new experiences.

They discovered joy in the simple pleasure of appreciating the beautiful scenery around them. Nature became a source of solace and inspiration as they immersed themselves in its tranquil embrace. Through those shared experiences, they developed a profound appreciation for life and the wonders that surrounded them.

In addition to their individual efforts to manage their mental health, Dave and Claire decided to join a local mental health group. Through this group, they had the pleasure of meeting some truly fantastic and interesting individuals. They made it a point to attend every week, engaging in various activities such as playing games like bingo and quizzes, sharing meals, and practising meditation. What was remarkable about this group was that it comprised individuals with diverse backgrounds and challenges. It wasn't solely for people with depression, the other members came from different walks of life. For instance, one lady in the group experienced water toxicity due to excessive water consumption, which caused her brain cells to swell and resulted in some brain damage. There were also seven attendees with unique needs including autism, learning difficulties, and mobility disabilities.

Dave and Claire genuinely enjoyed the time they spent with these individuals. They embraced the opportunity to connect with people who had different life experiences and challenges. Being part of this group had enriched their lives and provided them with a sense of community and support. All in all, Dave and Claire found themselves in a great place in life. They actively prioritised their mental health while also embracing the company and camaraderie of the mental health group, where they met remarkable friends and engaged in fulfilling activities.

CHAPTER 32

~WHEN HOPE GROWS~

Life in a few years....

Marcus utilised his time at home to develop his knowledge, particularly in IT. He developed a brilliant mind with a heart full of compassion. He had always believed in the power of technology to bring people together and make the world a better place. With that vision in mind, he set out on a mission to create a 'Help App' that would revolutionise the way people communicated and supported one another. After a couple of years, with his hard work and dedication, Marcus finally unveiled his creation to the world. The app, named "Global Helps", quickly gained popularity and became a beacon of hope for those in need, much to his amazement. It connected people from all corners of the globe, allowing them to lend a helping hand to their fellow human beings.

Among the many who were touched by Marcus's invention was Kay. Kay had always been passionate about helping others but felt limited in her corporate job. When she heard about Global Helps, she knew she wanted to be part of her husband's work. Without hesitation, she left her job and dedicated herself to supporting Marcus and promoting his work. As Marcus and Kay worked side by side, their love for each other grew stronger. Their son, Arlo, watched with admiration as his father's app changed the lives of countless individuals.

Arlo was immensely proud of his dad's achievements, and he too, felt the call to make a difference in the world. He pursued his dreams and became a lawyer, using his legal expertise to fight for justice and equality. Marcus and Kay beamed with pride as they witnessed their son's accomplishments, knowing that their own values had been passed down to the next generation. Time flew by, and one day, Arlo and his wife gave Marcus and Kay the most precious gift of all—a beautiful grandson named Marco. The arrival of little Marco filled their lives with pure joy and love. As they held the tiny bundle close to their hearts, they realised that the pain they had once experienced from an awful tragedy had transformed into a magical and transformative journey. Together as a family, they celebrated each milestone, cherishing the moments of laughter, love, and togetherness. The tragedy that had once cast a shadow over their lives was now a distant memory, replaced by the radiant light of hope and happiness. And so, the story of Marcus, Kay, Arlo, and little Marco became an inspiration to many. It taught the world that even in the face of adversity, love and determination can create something beautiful.

Through their work, they brought people together, fostered connections, and made the world a brighter place.

Sudi and her family...

Their lives were forever changed when their beloved Manjit passed away. The pain of losing her was indescribable, and the couple found themselves wading through the depths of grief with emotions that ebbed and flowed like the tides.

In the darkness of their sorrow, Sudi and Dhrav made a heartfelt promise to their daughter. They vowed to honour her memory by embarking on a journey to all the places in the UK that she had loved and cherished. From the rolling hills of the countryside to the bustling streets of London, they sought familiarity in the steps Manjit had once taken. They even expanded their horizons and ventured abroad, exploring the destinations their daughter had longed to visit. Together, they learned to enjoy life again, cherishing the moments they had left and hoping that their daughter looked down upon them with pride.

As they travelled from one place to another, Sudi and Dhrav found themselves gradually healing. Each picturesque landscape and vibrant cityscape seemed to whisper to their souls, reminding them of the beauty their daughter had cherished. They discovered that by immersing themselves in the wonders of the world, they were able to channel their grief into a bittersweet appreciation for life. While Dhrav found peace in spending time tending to his garden, Sudi sought a different kind of connection.

Late at night, when the world was quiet and still, she

would sit by the window and find herself drawn to writing letters. These letters were addressed to Sarah, Manjit's partner who had shared a deep and profound love with her daughter. Through these heartfelt exchanges Sudi and Sarah formed an unbreakable bond, united in their grief and their enduring love for Manjit.

With each letter, memories and stories of Manjit came to life. Sudi and Sarah laughed and cried together as they shared anecdotes, discovering new facets of Manjit's life that they hadn't known before. These revelations brought warmth to their hearts and painted vivid pictures of the vibrant spirit that their daughter had possessed. Days turned into months, and months into years. Sudi found comfort in their shared memories and the newfound friendship that had blossomed between them. Their connection became a lifeline, a source of strength that helped them guide the challenges of their grief.

As the years passed, Sudi and Dhrav found themselves growing too old. Their bodies became weary, and their spirits longed for the day they would be reunited with their beloved daughter. They looked forward to the next world, where they believed they would find light and eternal happiness in Manjit's presence. And so, as the sun set on their lives, Sudi and Dhrav held onto their memories and their love for Manjit. With hearts full of gratitude for the time they had shared on Earth, they took their final breaths, knowing that their journey was complete. They prayed to see their daughter once more, hoping to find peace in her loving embrace.

As their souls ascended, the world they left behind was forever touched by the story of Sudi and Dhrav, a testament to the enduring power of love, loss, and the unbreakable bonds that connect us all.

Dave and Claire had been together for many years and continued building their love for one another. However, their lives took a heartbreaking turn when Dave fell ill with a persistent cough and fatigue that seemed to linger for months. Claire, being a caring and attentive partner, grew increasingly concerned about Dave's health. She urged him to seek medical help, hoping that it was just a minor illness that could be easily treated. Reluctantly, Dave finally decided to listen to Claire's pleas and scheduled an appointment with a doctor.

The news they received was devastating. Dave was diagnosed with stage 4 lung cancer, and the doctors informed him that his life was limited to just a few months. The weight of this diagnosis crushed Claire's heart. She couldn't fathom the thought of losing the love of her life, the person who had been her rock and source of strength, the only happiness she'd ever known. In her anguish, Claire made a solemn declaration to Dave. She told him that she couldn't bear the thought of living without him and that she would join him in passing away together.

Her pain was so intense that she believed death was the only way to escape the impending loss. But Dave, even in the face of his own mortality, had a different perspective. He knew how much Claire meant to him, and he couldn't bear the thought of her sacrificing her own life with his. With a gentle voice and tears in his eyes, he encouraged Claire to live and find happiness even after he was gone.

Dave reminded Claire of the pain they had experienced before they found each other. He spoke of the trials they had overcome, the obstacles they had faced, and the strength they had gained from those experiences. He assured her that life had a way of working out, and although they were being tested in the most difficult way, they had the power to overcome it. Through his words, Dave reminded Claire of the incredible love they shared and how it had brought immense joy into their lives. He encouraged her to hold onto that love, cherish their memories, and find hope in the belief that something amazing could come out of even the darkest of times. Claire listened to Dave's words, and although her heart still ached with pain, she wanted to support his decision. She realised that Dave's love would always be with her, guiding her through the difficult days ahead. She vowed to honour his memory by living a life filled with purpose and positivity.

In the months that followed, Dave's health declined rapidly, but Claire stood by his side, holding his hand and providing comfort until his final breath. It was an incredibly difficult and traumatic farewell, but Dave's words continued to echo in her heart, reminding her to be strong and face the future with courage. Despite experiencing profound grief and loss, she made the brave decision to seek medical help and engage in regular sessions with a grief counsellor. This showed her willingness to confront her emotions and actively work towards healing.

As time went on, Claire's healing journey led to her becoming a mental health advocate and speaker. Embracing a leadership role in the mental health groups allowed her to use her own experiences and story to support and inspire others who were going through similar circumstances. This role gave her the opportunity to travel around the UK, meeting and helping countless individuals who suffered from grief and depression. By sharing her story and offering guidance, she became a source of hope and encouragement for others, making a positive impact on their lives.

She often worked with groups of people who seemed to have lost their way, as if they drifted through life like shadows, their faces imprinted with sorrow and their hearts burdened with the force of emptiness. For them, happiness seemed to be an elusive dream, and love was nothing more than a mirage in the desert of existence. Claire couldn't help but feel an ache of sadness for them, as if she was experiencing the same emptiness that had once plagued her own life. Claire was adamant about bringing a gleam of hope back into their world. She inflamed inspiration within countless individuals.

As a result, profound transformations began to unfold. From the depths of despair, Claire magically sparked gifts of hope, which had ignited in them, spreading like wildfire through the hearts of the once joyless souls. Although Claire chose not to pursue romantic love again after losing Dave, she found fulfilment and joy in her advocacy work. Filling the void in her heart and mind, meeting and connecting with people who shared similar struggles allowed her to understand them deeply and motivate them to find their own path to healing. Achieving this was no small accomplishment. It presented immense difficulties and often required Claire to step out of her comfort zone, even when she longed to retreat from society. Her inspiration was her profound love for Dave and the impact he had on her life.

She never stopped loving him. He had left an indelible mark on her heart, forever engraved within the deepest corners of her being. His laughter continued to illuminate her soul, acting as a guiding light in her darkest moments. The memories they had shared together became intertwined with her hopes and dreams for the future, serving as a constant reminder of what they had once had. He remained a burning light in her soul. The love she held for him endured a profound connection that transcended time and space.

THE END

Thank you for reading. Please consider leaving a review.

Author's Note

In the depth of my anguish, I found myself reflecting on the curious paradoxes of life. 'Why is it?' I wondered, 'that we only truly appreciate the value of something when we stand on the precipice of losing it? Why is it that the prospect of death compels us to seek meaning and purpose in life with a newfound urgency?'

As I contemplated my thoughts, life presented her with yet another sorrowful chapter. I received the news that my beloved mother was facing an imminent death after being diagnosed with advanced lung cancer. The thought of losing my mother, my confidante, and best friend, was inconceivable. My heart shattered into a million pieces, for my mother had been a beacon of light in my life, and the thought of a world without her seemed unbearable. The grief that wrapped my soul was immense, as I struggled to come to terms with the reality of my impending loss.

As I sat by my mother's bedside, holding her fragile hand, I realised the answers to these questions were woven into the fabric of human nature. It is in the face of loss and mortality that we are jolted out of our complacency, forced to confront the fleeting nature of our existence. We become acutely aware of the preciousness of time and the fragility of the relationships we hold dear. I recalled the times when I had taken my mother's presence for granted, assuming that I would always be there. I wasn't prepared for the death of my mother. I remembered the missed opportunities to express my love and gratitude, the moments when I had been too preoccupied with my own concerns to fully appreciate the depth of my mother's love.

Regret washed over me like a relentless tide, but within the sorrow, a flame of hope flickered within my heart. I made a solemn vow to honour my mother's legacy by cherishing every moment, by embracing the people I loved, and by living a life of purpose and meaning.

I built my life by focusing on the positive aspects, as I continued to

grapple with the loss of my mother. I directed my energy towards my passion for writing and I successfully completed my very first, feature film - screenplay. I surprisingly became an award-winning screenwriter.

This brought immense joy and a sense of achievement to myself. Something I desperately needed at that time.

Then unexpectedly, I crossed paths with someone who was truly extraordinary. I had discovered the love of my life, my soul partner who ignited a fire within me. Every fibre of her being adored and cherished her lover. I embraced every aspect of my partner, both the good and the bad, recognising that imperfections were part of what made their love so real and authentic. My partner became my world, a source of joy and support that seemed unparalleled. Burt Darcy possessed a vibrant and compassionate nature that seemed to breathe new life into my weary soul.

From the moment we connected, there was an undeniable spark between us—a deep resonance that went beyond the boundaries of our own individual struggles.

The connection we had was like an eclipse of light, that transcended the limits of magic. I had found acceptance and a sense of belonging that I had longed for my entire life. However, as time went on, the clash of differences and the challenges we both faced due to each other's adversities with ADHD and autism, began to cast a shadow over our relationship. These obstacles grew insurmountable, creating a divide that seemed impossible to bridge, no matter how pure and genuine our love was.

It was a heartbreaking realisation that love alone sometimes cannot overcome the complexities of life. The loss of my relationship left a painful hole in my heart, a constant reminder that even the most profound love can falter under the weight of circumstances. It was a sobering lesson that despite our deep connection, sometimes external factors and personal challenges can create barriers that are simply too great to overcome.

In the centre of my broken heart, I was forced to confront the harsh reality that love does not always guarantee a happily ever after. It was a valuable lesson that taught me the fragility of relationships and the importance of acknowledging and addressing the obstacles that arise along the way.

As I mourned the loss of what I believed was my forever love, I set out on a journey of self-reflection and self-discovery, revealing that my worth and capacity to love deeply were not defined by the end of my relationship. I learned to embrace my strengths and quirks, understanding that my struggles were part of my unique journey.

The sound of words flowed from my mind to the paper, I felt a sense of liberation. Writing became my therapy, helping me navigate through the depths of my sadness and heal the wounds within my heart. Every sentence I penned was a step towards healing, a way to reclaim my sense of self. I dedicated myself to overcome the personal and mental health challenges that had hindered my progress in life. Recognising the need for assistance, I sought help from medical professionals, relied on medication when necessary, and surrounded myself with a supportive network. My consistent tenacity pushed my pursuit of self-improvement and personal growth, all to feel deserving of unconditional love.

In addition to addressing my broken self, I understood the importance of nurturing my creative spirit. Embracing my love for writing, I continued to channel my pain and heartache into my passion. Through the act of writing, my heart and mind found consolation, working in tandem to escape the grip of dark thoughts. Gradually, I began to heal, progressively through my sadness and eventually transforming my heart into a novel. Months passed, and my dedication and perseverance has hopefully paid off. The culmination of my efforts emerged in the form of a book titled: 'The Best Death.'

About the Author

Shalina Casey is an award-winning actress and screenwriter. She has been working in the film industry for some years and has worked very hard to become an established actress in TV and Film. Writing is where her heart and soul are, and she is ambitiously determined to become a successful writer.

Within the last couple of years, she has won several awards for two feature film screenplays, earning her several credits for 'Best Feature Film Screenplay.'

Awards [Page Turner Prize | British Urban Film Festival (BUFF) KinoDrome: International | Chicago International Film Festival | London International Film Festival | LGTBQ Unboarded International Film Festival | British Urban Film Festival (BUFF)]

https://m.imdb.com/name/nm11564793/

Printed in Great Britain
by Amazon

46155748R00162